NECROMANCER

JAY TUCKERMAN

For everyone who fails to appreciate how their life affects so many others

Hal Carmody was always fast. Almost a month fast getting out of his mother's womb. Fast on his knees, then his feet, then his bicycle, roller skates, skate board. As a track star at Lincoln High, he had not lost a race in the 400, 800 or 1500 meters in three years. At six-two and about a hundred and forty pounds, Hal was all legs and bones, light as the wind he was often compared to. Given his build, track and ping-pong were as close to contact sports as he dared.

Still, having set the state record for the 800 and not far off the mark for the 400 and 1500, Hal was already being courted for scholarships by some of the best track and field universities. Heading into his senior year, he was interested in USC, UCLA and Stanford, hoping that his girlfriend Becca would get into one or more of those schools so they could be together. Becca, she of the unruly red hair and emerald-green eyes, freckles galore, what Hal would classify as "goofy-cute," was a good field hockey player and decent student, but not a lock on either front to get a free ride somewhere.

Hal's best friend, Mike Barber, was every girl's and mother's dream, a straight A student, Clooney-handsome, super-polite, and a two-letter man, star wide receiver for the football team and lights-out pitcher for the baseball squad. Mike's future was so bright, as the song goes, he had to wear shades.

Hal and Mike had known each other since they were infants, as the Barbers and Carmodys lived on the same street and the boys attended the same schools since kindergarten, swam at the same club, and played for the same little league team (sponsored by Vito's Pizza!). Frank and Melody Carmody, Hal's folks, were also close friends with Mark and Marcy Barber. The families went on holidays together, and Hal's younger sisters Alison and Petra (fourteen and permanently affixed to her iPhone) got on well with Mike's younger brother Thom and his sister Caroline.

Unlike the families Hal saw on TV or read about in books, his was relatively mundane and peaceful. No major blowups, no unexpected pregnancies, no alcoholic parent. Just microwave popcorn and movies, the occasional spirited game of Scrabble or Risk or Monopoly, some penny-ante poker games. And even when there might have been a major row, such as the time they found Hal's computer contained some highly-adult material or when they discovered half a joint in Petra's music box, his parents were so steady and unflappable that those incidents were dealt with by a calm discussion about masturbation being nothing to be embarrassed about (talk about embarrassment!) and that pot was likely to interfere with the things (both social and academic) that would help determine Petra's future. Although they had a little of that self-help generation lameness about them, Hal appreciated that he was treated as being on equal footing rather than a child to be scolded or corrected.

In addition to Mike, Hal's other partner in crime was Seth Wildman, whose nickname was therefore by default "The Wild Man." This was a misnomer in every sense of the word, as Seth could charitably be described as a quintessential geek. Black framed glasses with lenses usually found only in an old folks home, braces that as far as anyone could remember had been there since infancy, a buzz cut mandated by his ex-Marine dad (Semper Fi!) and an already impressive beer gut before his first beer. Seth's primary redeeming quality was that he was hilarious. He had a photographic memory for jokes, and thus he was always armed with a least a few good ones for any occasion.

Case in point: The three boys were having an after school snack at Vito's, which they frequented because (a) it was on the way home; (b) pizza was cheap; (c) Vito's was the life blood of the Lincoln little league team and (d) because Vito's daughter Jean, who worked behind the counter, was drool-worthy. Mike had gotten some loot for his birthday and so was treating the three of them to slices and sodas. As they settled into the corner booth, with its comforting but cracking red vinyl cushions inexpertly repaired with duct tape, Seth, with hot pizza in his mouth, started in. "Okay, I got one! (Chewing interruption)... So these two guys meet on the street. They haven't seen each other in twenty years. The one guy says 'Hey, John, I haven't seen you in ages! How are you?' John replies 'I...almost...got...married.' So the other guy says 'Wow, you lost your stutter! You used to have such a terrible time of it.' John says 'the...doctor...told...me...that...if...I...talk...slowly...I ...won't...stutter.' The other guy says 'That's great! So what's this about you almost getting married?' John says 'my...fiancée... and... I... were... sitting... on... the... porch... and... she... was... scratching... her... dog... behind... the... ears..., and... I... said... that...

when...we...get...married...she...could...do...that...for...me.

She...got...up...and...threw...the...ring...in...my...face ...and...stormed...off...and...I...never...saw...her...again.' The other guy says 'Man, that's crazy! I don't understand why she would get so mad about that?' John says 'by...the...time...I...had...finished...talking...the...dog ...was...licking...his... balls.'"

Soda through the nose for Mike, near Heimlich maneuver required for me as I was choking on my pizza from laughing so hard. Once I caught my breath I noticed Mrs. Fisher in the booth across from us giving me the eyes of death. As usual, Seth was the last to stop laughing even though it was his joke.

I left the two of them to head home, as I had a meet the next day and yet the school still had the nerve to expect me to do homework! I will not be dedicating my Olympic gold medals to Principal Frobisher. Speaking of dogs, our pit bull Maya greeted me at the door with her usual level of enthusiasm. If only Jean felt the same way about me. Pit bulls get a bit of a bad rap due to all the bad people out there that train them to be mean and to fight, but Maya is about the sweetest dog you would ever want to meet. Big head, muscular and grey, with those eyes that say I worship the ground you walk on. She's even okay around other dogs. Not to say she particularly *likes* them, but she ignores them unless they get too close to her personal space (i.e. her butthole).

My parents are always on about how great it is to be a kid these days, how they never had Xbox or Blu Ray or iPads or phones that do somersaults, but actually I think it makes it much harder. To hear them tell it, they had a TV and a record player and that was it, and they could only play or watch at designated times. But when I come home from school, I can (a) play Call of Duty or Madden; (b) watch Lord of the Rings on Blu Ray (for about the hundredth time); (c) surf hilarious videos on You Tube; or (d) do the dry, boring, mind-numbing homework courtesy of Lincoln High. And even when I muster the self-discipline to choose (d), the constant pinging and buzzing of my phone is like a siren's call to the rocks of summer school.

So this is my entirely plausible excuse for hanging on to a B- grade average by my fingernails. Fortunately the folks are not these "my child must conquer the world at all costs" types of parents, and so we share a sort of mutual malaise about my grades. Which isn't to say they don't care. My mom is a top litigator at Wheeler, Dealer and Schemer (as we jokingly refer to the firm), and dad is a professor at Morgan State, teaching physics to the two Russians in his class who, according to dad, actually have the capacity to understand what the hell he is talking about. So no dummies in the Carmody clan. But they have this karmic attitude that all will work out in the end, so they don't bust my chops about being in the fifty-first percentile.

Alison and Petra are better students, and despite her obsession with Facebook, Twitter and Instagram (and who knows what else), Petra aces just about everything. If it wasn't for track, I might see if those joints actually make you smarter! Alison is a sweet kid, not yet non-communicative due to device addiction, and she has a real sense of wonder about the world. She loves watching nature programs and even bizarrely seems to have an interest in what dad does. Much as I love Maya, I think Alison would die if something happened to her, and vice-versa.

CHAPTER TWO

Sid Mackey was on a losing streak. Unfortunately for Sid, it was going on twenty years. It wasn't always that way for Sid. He had a great job with Union Auto, the world's most understanding wife in June, and a great group of friends from the plant and from his time in the Army. Sid served seven years with the armed services, saw some combat, and was honorably discharged after taking shrapnel in his knee and thigh after an IAD exploded.

After coming home from military service, Sid met June at, of all places, Lincoln Raceway. June was on a girls' day out at the races, putting on her two dollar wagers and rooting for the horse she randomly chose. She saw Sid making various notations in his Racing Form and asked him what he was doing. He explained that he was looking at the horses' past performances, whether they ran better on a dry or wet track, whether they preferred the dirt or the turf, whether they were good at the distance the race would be run, and so on. To his surprise, June was fascinated by the discussion and prodded him for more information. They ultimately agreed to a lunch date so he could further explain the nuances of handicapping horses. Thus was the start of a great romance.

That lunch turned into dinners and movies and eventually more intimate activities, along with several visits to the track, as they both enjoyed the thrill of the races. A few weeks before their wedding date, June and Sid were at Lincoln Raceway, looking at the entries in the sixth race. June suddenly screamed and pointed, "Look, Sid, there's a horse called Lucky's Bride running! We have to bet her!" Sid looked at the chart for Lucky's Bride and, to put it kindly, she was a dog. Never came in better than fifth in any race (out of a field of six), slow as molasses, in with much more expensive horses and running a distance she had never run before. Sid took a peek at the current odds on the board and saw she was 62-1, which struck him as about right. But never one to argue with a woman's intuition, he made a two dollar win wager for June and threw the horse in a trifecta box for himself, just in case.

As the horses rounded the clubhouse turn, two of the horses Sid had put in his trifecta were on or near the lead. Predictably, Lucky's Bride was languishing in seventh, reminding Sid of an old horse player's joke ("She went off at five to one and came in at 2:15"). Suddenly, as if some divine force were propelling her, Lucky's Bride began weaving between horses, making up chunks of ground. Moving to fifth, then third, then second. As the wire approached, she was neck and neck with a horse named Mistral, and it was too close to call. A photo finish was flashed on the tote board. June was jumping up and down like a schoolgirl. After a considerable delay, the tote board finally showed the order of finish—Lucky's Bride first, Mistral second and Rodeo Gal third. Lucky's Bride paid $126.00 to win, and June screamed as if she had just won the lottery. But with Mistral coming second at 7-1 and Rodeo Gal coming third at 11-1, the trifecta payout was $11,876. Sid triumphantly showed his winning ticket to June and then pointed at the tote board, and the expression on June's face was priceless, like a goldfish gasping for air.

Although there was no way he could have realized it at the time, amidst all the euphoria of the BIG WIN, that moment was the beginning of the end of Sid's happy life. Not in any abrupt way, but rather in a slow, cancerous downward spiral of gambling and lying and self-hatred.

Due largely to the BIG WIN, June and Sid were able to take an extravagant honeymoon in the South of France, staying in a luxurious hotel and mingling among the beautiful people. Sid would never be mistaken for one of them, with his baggy eyes and boxer's nose, but June fit in perfectly, like a little pixie, with a Dorothy Hamill cut, pert little upturned nose and pretty cornflower eyes. Sid was constantly amazed that she had somehow found herself attracted to him. While in Cannes, they took a side trip to Monte Carlo, and Sid did his best, if nonetheless weak, James Bond impression at the famous casino there.

When they returned to the states, Sid went back to his job managing a line crew at Union Auto, and June her job as a secretary at an accounting firm. They were by no means wealthy, but with two decent incomes and no kids, they were comfortable. They had tried to have children, but after a period without success, June went to the doctor and was told that because of an anomaly with her womb, she would be unable to conceive. Devastated, she cried for hours on end, and all Sid could do was hug her and tell her they still had each other. After, they talked many times about adoption, but never got around to following through with the idea.

Sid had mixed feelings about the "children issue." On the one hand, he thought it would be great to build a family with June, and he was positive that she would make a great mother. But his interactions with most families and their little brats left him a bit cold about the whole thing. These kids were nothing like the polite TV version of children he grew up with. Rather, they were generally throwing fits whenever they did not get their way, or sullen and unresponsive. He did meet some genuinely nice kids, but being a man used to calculating the odds, he was thinking longshot. But for June's sake, he would have happily tossed those concerns aside.

The Union Auto plant was only about fifteen minutes from the track, and on occasion Sid would go on a lunchtime to bet a couple races. After the BIG WIN, however, Sid found himself at the track on a more frequent basis, making excuses about doctor appointments or a sick relative to absent himself for hours at a time. Worse, he was betting larger amounts as time went on, perhaps subconsciously trying to recreate that glorious moment with June. He even tried thinking like her, looking for cute names of horses and betting them even when they were dogs. At first, he wasn't particularly concerned about the money, as their expenses were mainly limited to mortgage and car payments, and they did not lead an extravagant life. That changed over time as Sid dug a bigger and bigger hole for himself. When he and June went to the races together, he was careful to behave himself, betting small amounts so that, win or lose, it was not a big deal.

If you asked him, Sid could not pinpoint the moment when the slide into oblivion began in earnest, but a good candidate would have been when he began to take money from their emergency fund and sometimes June's purse. At first, June would comment on the missing money and Sid would scratch his head and feign ignorance. Later, June wouldn't bother acknowledging the missing money, resigned to what was going on. So the self-loathing of being a thief in his own home was surpassed only by the increasing depression Sid felt at constantly losing more and more money at the track. For a long time, he was good at hiding those feelings, coming home with a chipper attitude, big smile and hug for June. "Yeah, great day hon, how about you?" Eventually, though, he got worn down by the money troubles and depression and self-hatred, and he could not hide those feelings from June even as he tried to do so.

Then June got sick and everything changed. At first she just felt woozy, lacking energy, tired all the time. Finally she went to see a doctor and after about a hundred tests, the diagnosis was a rare form of leukemia. The next three years involved every possible treatment option, from chemo to non-traditional. June was a fighter and hung on gamely, even as she began to lose her hair and to age prematurely as a result of the highly intrusive treatment methods. And even in the worst and most agonizing times for her, when the pain was beyond what she thought humanly possible, she always put on a brave and smiling face for Sid.

Between the co-pays and uncovered treatments and Sid's continuing streak of losses at the track, the Mackeys were forced to sell their home and moved into a one bedroom apartment in a so-called "transitional" neighborhood, meaning that daytime activities were reasonably safe, but best to be tucked away with triple locks engaged by ten at night. As their social life was vastly limited by June's condition and lack of money, this was not much of a problem. Old friends and neighbors dropped by on occasion, but as June's condition worsened, those visits became less frequent. Sid understood, since if he could have avoided the personal hell of seeing this once vibrant creature deteriorate into a shell of herself, he probably would have too.

Sid spent less time at the track, since he needed to be there for June whenever possible, and because he just couldn't afford to keep losing. Still, he managed to find twenty or forty bucks to put a few wagers on at lunchtime during the work week. Sid had never been what anyone would call a heavy drinker, but the combination of the financial woes and June's state did see him increasingly seeking the shelter of a numbing buzz.

In February of the following year June's condition took a major turn for the worse. The pain was constant and unbearable, and even the painkillers and morphine drip did little to make her comfortable. If she were an animal, the vet no doubt would have told Sid that the humane thing to do would be to put her to sleep. Eventually they moved her to a hospice care center where Sid stayed by her side every moment he was not working. June, sensing the end was near, beckoned for Sid to come closer and whispered in his ear "Darling, I want you to promise me that you will go on living for both of us with the same spirit we had when we were together. I know you have done some not so great things, but I forgive you and I want you to forgive yourself. Hopefully I am going to a better place, maybe not if God is keeping track of my church attendance. But know that I have always loved you and always will."

After Sid managed to control his tears, he whispered back to June, "I'm sorry I was not a better husband to you. I tried to be good but I was weak and selfish. You deserved more than any man could give you, and if I had the chance to do it again I would make any sacrifice just to see that smile on your face one more time. I'm scared to death of going on without you but I will try to honor your love and spirit in everything I do. And I will find you again no matter what it takes." Sid kissed her on her forehead and watched her fall asleep for the last time.

After the grief counselors and the funeral directors and the coffee and cake with the mourners, with their well-meaning but ultimately useless words of comfort, Sid was alone once again. The small life insurance policy paid for the funeral and remaining medical bills, and they had adapted to being a one income family once June had to stop working. Sid tried gamely to keep his chin up and to honor June's wishes, but the sorrow and loneliness ate at his spirit until he too was a shell of his former self.

Sid fell back upon the only means of forgetting and insulating himself-drinking and betting. He and June used to laugh about those ads with checklists to determine whether you had a "drinking problem." "Do you often drink alone?" "Do you have your first drink before noon?" Increasingly, Sid fit the prototype for a problem drinker. Although on rare occasion he still got together with some of their old friends, he found that all it did was remind him of June's absence, so he stopped socializing altogether, except with his new friends (as the joke goes) Johnny Walker and Jim Beam.

Any spare money Sid managed to find went to Lincoln Raceway. Like most gamblers, Sid had the occasional good day sandwiched around multiple bad ones. Still, the thrill of the races was a temporary reprieve from his otherwise gloomy existence. Never again did he experience the magic of the BIG WIN as he had with June. He even tried to pick horses she would have chosen (Cindy's Pumpkin, Fleet Unicorn, Pixie Dust), but never found the miracle finishes. Because the booze at the track would have eaten into his limited betting fund, he managed to stay sober while at the races. It reminded him of a particularly ironic joke given his circumstances, where a gambler asks his friend for money so that his wife can have a life-saving operation. When the friend says that he would give him the money, except that he knows the guy will just gamble it way, the guy says "No, I *have* gambling money!"

As a reasonably functional drinker and compulsive gambler, Sid managed to balance his vices with his work obligations, at least for a while. But as time went on, the absences due to drinking or a can't miss bet became more frequent. After several warnings, Sid was called into his boss's office one morning in August. Also present was a woman he recognized from the Human Resources department. Not a good sign. His Boss, Frank Johnson, looked uncomfortable and finally said, "Sid, I'm sorry but we have to let you go. Your attendance has become a major problem, and you were warned more than once that this could not continue. And there have been other complaints as well about your behavior on the line, and....other things. I always liked you and I wish things could be different but we have a business to run and I need people I can count on. Ms. Harlow will explain your severance package and the job assistance programs that Union provides. Good luck to you, Sid."

Sid tried to be angry with Frank but in his heart knew that he had probably been overly generous or sympathetic to his circumstances, in letting him stay on this long. After Ms. Harlow antiseptically explained his severance package (twelve weeks of salary, two months of continued medical benefits, sixty days of placement assistance consulting, etc.), Sid was escorted to collect his personal belongings and waved goodbye to his co-workers as he left the plant for the last time, with several of them promising to get together soon, even as they knew this would not happen.

After so many years working at Union, Sid thought it would hit him harder, but the shell he had built around himself after June's death left him largely immune to much by way of emotion. Since although under less than ideal circumstances Sid had the rest of the day free, he dropped off his stuff at home, grabbed a Racing Form at the local news agent, and headed to the track.

Sid's three month severance managed to last him nearly two, a small miracle in light of his booze consumption and wagering. Although he was not old enough to tap into his retirement account at Union, he began to do so, notwithstanding the hefty penalty, promising himself it was only a stop-gap measure until he found another job. The problem was that between his drinking and time at the track, he found little time or enthusiasm to apply for anything. And in the ever-evolving economy, the types of jobs Sid could legitimately say he was qualified for were few and far between. The small withdrawals from his 401K became incrementally larger over time. In desperation, he took a minimum wage job at a local MegaMart, along with the other fifty-somethings whose lives had gone horribly awry.

CHAPTER THREE

Eddie and Nancy Porter had been married for twenty-two years, and according to their separate but dazzlingly similar calculations, at least four of those had been happy. They had two boys, Sean, 15 and Marcus, 13. Outwardly, they were the prototypical happy American family. Behind the scenes, a different story emerged.

Eddie was a weatherman on the Channel 7 News ("Get out there and enjoy this beautiful spring weekend!") and Nancy was a stay at home mom. They got married not long after graduating from high school, despite the protests of both sets of parents that they were far too young to jump into marriage. Although at the time they casually discarded such advice, upon later reflection they realized that their parents may have been right. Not because they weren't mature enough to make the decision at the time, but because they exhausted so much of their youthful exuberance during the first few years of marriage, the remaining years began to feel more and more like an obligation rather than an adventure. To try and remedy this, they decided to have children, and Sean and Marcus followed in fairly close order. At first, the euphoria and terror of becoming parents did bring a newfound excitement into their lives, and the myriad of tasks associated with babies kept them preoccupied pretty much twenty-four/seven.

Over time, and not without a touch of irony, they realized that their decision to have children had turned their marriage into even more of an obligation. They loved both kids very much, and Sean and Marcus, on the scale of Jesus/Bad Seed were pretty good boys. But the effort put into planning and saving and taking care of the boys ultimately sapped whatever sense of passion Ed and Nancy had left for each other. It wasn't that they actively disliked each other. As with most marriages, there were lots of little things that annoyed the other partner, such as Eddie's unfortunate farting problem or that he cracked his knuckles way too often and too loudly. Or Nancy's cracking of her gum when she talked or her habit of commenting upon how many beers Eddie had consumed in a particular evening. If asked, either would do anything to protect the other, and there was still an undercurrent of love and respect between the two. But as passion had left the building much like Elvis, the marriage became more like a humorless friendship than anything else.

Another irony was that although both spouses were one-hundred percent faithful to each other, there were constant nagging suspicions on both sides that the other was having an affair. This was of course left unspoken and unquestioned, as to bring up the subject would be the equivalent of marital nuclear war, with no going back whatever the answer. But the question remained in the back of their minds as the sex became less and less frequent and they both wondered how the other was filling the void.

On the plus side, Eddie and Nancy had an active circle of friends. The closest were Bert and Melinda Baylor, who they both knew from high school and who had also chosen to settle down in

Lincoln. Bert was a major league prospect at catcher for the Phillies until his knee blew out during a game and the repairs were not enough to sustain the rigors of the position. He was a burly (going on obese) man with a bemused attitude towards pretty much everything. Never bitter about not making it to the pros, always demurring that he was never a good enough hitter to make it in the bigs ("couldn't hit a curveball to save my life"), he opened what was now the only remaining sporting goods store in downtown Lincoln and had a successful business. Melinda was the quintessential cheerleader, bubbly and blond and button-nose cute. She had turned her high school bake sale fundraising skills into a gourmet cupcake business, still amazed that people would pay three dollars for fifteen cents worth of sugar and flour.

Bert and Melinda were the antidote to Eddie and Nancy's automaton existence, and they got together with the couple whenever possible. They even went on vacations together, which, according to Nancy, was the ultimate test of the strength of a friendship. She was the voice of experience on the subject, having made the mistake of travelling with marginal friends who quickly became sworn enemies, either by using up all the hot water in the shower or wanting to go to some idiotic tourist trap or wanting to split the dinner bill down to the nearest atom. But Bert and Melinda were so easy-going and fun that it was a joy to have them along on any trip. And as a bonus, Bert and Melinda's two boys, Eric and Nick, were fast friends with their own kids.

But after twenty-two years, the little irritations and suspicions and resentments had become firmly cemented, and so they settled into a stage of mutually assured tolerance, not exactly fighting on a regular basis but always seemingly on the edge, with both parties trying to probe just how far they could go before initiating the type of uncomfortable exchange they were both desperately trying to avoid.

CHAPTER FOUR

So far, Hal's senior year track season had been a smashing success. He had lost only one race, the 400, to a ridiculously fast kid from King High, and even that race was dead close. Otherwise, he was winning races by ever-increasing margins, and in the 1500 meter race last weekend the other participants were mere dots on the horizon. To celebrate his latest success, his parents took him, Mike and Seth to Burger Bistro, Hal's favorite restaurant. He ordered The Macho Burger, a coronary-inducing combination of ten ounces of beef, cheddar and blue cheese, onion rings, guacamole and hot sauce. Along with orders of fries and milkshakes, the boys were in burger heaven.

It was physically impossible for Seth to keep his mouth shut for more than a couple minutes at a time, and the urge to share his latest jokes was too much to contain. But he did vaguely understand the concept of "audience adaptation," and knowing Hal's folks were not overly keen on bad language or jokes involving sex, he dug into his vault of "family friendly jokes." "Okay, so these two ladies, Mary and Jane, have been friends their whole lives. They played softball in school together and have always stayed active. When they got old and Mary was close to dying, Jane came to visit and asked Mary to promise her that she would find a way to let her know about Heaven after she got there. Mary agreed that she would if she could. A few days after Mary died Jane was sleeping when suddenly she heard this eerie voice saying 'June, June.' June leapt up and said 'Who's there!' The voice said 'It's Mary.' June said 'You can't be Mary. Mary's dead!' The voice said 'It's me Jane, I'm in Heaven!' June said 'Oh my god, Mary, it's you! Tell me about Heaven.' Mary says, 'Oh, it's mostly wonderful, but I have a little bad news. We play softball every day and the fields are emerald green and the sky is perfectly blue. All our old friends from school are here and everybody is young again and we never get tired. It's a magical place!' June says, 'That sounds wonderful! You mentioned some bad news. What could possibly be bad up there?' And Mary replies 'You're pitching Tuesday.'"

Predictably, Mr. Carmody burst into gales of laughter, Mrs. Carmody gave a small tittering laugh and proclaimed "that's awful" with a smile on her face, and the boys groaned as they had heard this one from Seth on numerous occasions. As parents do when they run out of things to say, Mrs. Carmody asked Seth and Mike what their plans were. Seth jumped in straightaway, telling her that he was going to Syracuse to be a communications major, but his true calling was comedy, so she should look for him on Jimmy Kimmel or Conan O' Brien. Mike was more low-key, telling Hal's folks that he had not yet made a decision and that a lot would depend on where he got the best scholarship offer from and whether it was an athletic or academic one. Mike loved football and knew he was good enough to play for at least a mid-major college, but was also smart enough to recognize that the odds were extremely long on making it in the pros. And with more and more stories about head injuries and their impact,

Mike was starting to reconsider whether he wanted to play football at all.

Mrs. Carmody applauded Mike on his thoughtfulness and told Seth he should have a back-up plan just in case he was not the next Jerry Seinfeld. Seth scoffed at that, confident that he was already one of the funniest people on the planet. Both Mike and Hal rolled their eyes at that, and Hal said, "Not sure about that, Seth, but I can confirm you are already one of the funniest-looking people on the planet!"

After dinner, Hal arrived home to Maya's excited greeting, and she was thrilled when he brought out a piece of burger he had managed to smuggle out. She was whining for more treats when Melody scolded both of them, telling Hal "That dog will be as big as this house if you keep feeding her treats. The vet said she needs to be on a controlled diet." Both Hal and Maya looked contrite but silently eyed each other to confirm that the treats would continue, albeit in a more covert manner.

Hal's cell went off and saw it was Becca, so he retreated to the privacy of his room. As soon as he connected he had to pull the phone away from his ear as Becca shrieked "YESSSS! I got into UCLA! They're even giving me a partial scholarship for hockey. Must be pretty desperate, huh?" Hal told her how thrilled he was for her and that if he got a scholarship offer he would take it so the two of them could stay together. Hal had always had trouble approaching girls, and so he was grateful when Becca approached him after school one day two years ago to see if he wanted to get some pizza. They had eased into a relationship from that day forward, platonic and sort of tomboyish at first, but slowly developing into lust if not exactly romance.

From her end, Becca loved Hal's graceful, greyhound-like features and his easy-going ways, and never felt pressure to change her looks or the way she acted. In her mind, that was the perfect basis for a relationship. She also liked Mike and even obnoxious Seth, and her opinion of Hal was enhanced by the friends he surrounded himself with. Hal was not quite as enamored of Becca's pals Abagail and Brittany (in Hal's opinion any girl named Brittany warranted extreme caution), but they were okay in small doses, and Hal was rarely subjected to the girls' social events.

After finishing up the call with Becca, Hal told his folks the good news. Hal's dad said that was great news, but of course his mom, interjecting unwanted responsibility into the conversation, told Hal that he needed to focus on what was best for him as far as schools went. "I know you care a lot for Becca, hon. But young romance has a way of fading once you get out in the world, and I don't want you to limit your choices solely based on where Becca gets in. If you two are truly meant to be together than it will happen even if you wind up at different schools. They have these amazing new inventions like phones and cars and airplanes that let people stay in touch even when they are in different places!" Hal gave her a perfunctory chuckle and replied, "I hear you mom. But Becca's the only girl I care about, and it's important to me that we stay close. Anyway, let's see where I get in before we make a big deal of this."

Hal knew that despite his mom's protests that she and dad would ultimately let Hal make the decision himself. That's why they were such cool parents. The tough decision would be if Hal got a scholarship to Stanford, since it was such a good school, and he was pretty sure Becca would not get in there. But at least they would be in the same state.

His dad called down that Maya needed to go for a walk. Hal saw confirmation of this as Maya was doing her "I seriously need to go" dance by the front door. Hal grabbed one of the "doggie-doo" bags and put the leash on. They had not gotten ten feet from the door when Maya unloaded, with Hal thinking that burger might not have been such a great idea after all. As Hal went about the unpleasant task of collecting and depositing Maya's poop, he recalled a comedy routine where the comic said that if aliens landed on the planet and saw humans picking up dogshit they would assume that the dogs were the masters and the humans their slaves.

When he and Maya returned home (after Maya nearly dislocated Hal's shoulder chasing after a squirrel), Alison wanted to play air hockey. They had an ancient table down in the basement that Hal had gotten for his thirteenth birthday, which now barely puffed out enough air to move the puck around, but for some reason was Alison's favorite game. They descended into the cluttered basement, the default storage area for anything that would not fit into the garage. Hal plugged in the table and it wheezed slowly to life. They found the scarred orange puck and white bangers, and Hal as always tried to give Alison every opportunity to score goals since she derived a wholly out of proportion giddiness every time she scored off of Hal.

After letting her win a close 7-6 game (an art Hal had perfected of not making it too obvious he was letting her win), Hal was taken aback when Alison asked him what happened to people when they died. "Geez, Alison, where did that come from?"

She said there was a program where the brother and sister were arguing about it, with the sister saying that you went to heaven if you were good or hell if you were bad, and the brother saying that everybody wound up in the same place, being eaten by worms. Hal paused for a moment, not wanting to be responsible for some hefty psychiatric bill in the future, and finally responded. "Truthfully, Alison, I have no idea, nor do I think anyone else does. Until we're dead, there's no way to know, and once we're dead, it's kind of hard to communicate. Anyway, I think you have seventy or eighty years until you need to worry about it." He grabbed her sides and tickled her until she was screaming and running up the stairs.

Allison's question continued to gnaw at Hal through the evening. Like most boys his age, religion was not high on his list of priorities. Although he accompanied his folks to church on the major holidays, he rarely paid much attention to the goings on. He had not formed any firm opinions about the existence of God. Like most people, he wanted to believe that some higher being was looking out for him, but with all the sad news he saw on television and the internet he had his doubts. His parents, to their credit, had never tried to cram their beliefs into him, and, come to think of it, he really had never discussed the subject with them.

So it came as a bit of a shock to them when, on their way to Costco to pick up a couple hundred rolls of toilet paper, Hal asked them if they believed in God. Both were silent for a moment, and his dad finally said "Speaking for myself, I do believe in God. It's purely a matter of faith, and that's why your mom and I have never made a big deal of it to you or the girls. Lots of good and bad things happen in life, and I don't think God controls those, as he gave man free will to chart his own course. So I don't think much of those athletes who say they owe their victories to God. It's their hard work and dedication and talent that get them where they are." Hal thought his dad's response was pretty reasonable, and took his mom's silence as acquiescence to his dad's position.

The next day, when he and Mike and Seth were having lunch at the McDonald's near the high school, Hal brought up Alison's out of the blue question. Of course this reminded Seth of a joke. "Okay, so there's this lawyer that dies and goes up to heaven and St. Peter meets him at the gates and welcomes him to heaven and explains that he gets to spend a day in heaven and a day in hell to decide where he wants to spend eternity. So the lawyer spends the day in heaven, floating on clouds and listening to harps, and tells St. Peter how nice it is. St. Peter nods and waves his hands and the next thing he knows the lawyer is in hell. He looks around and guys are playing poker and golf and watching beautiful women dancing naked and smoking cigars. The next morning he's back in heaven and St. Peter asks him where he wants to spend eternity. The lawyer says 'St. Peter, I'm honored that you would have me in heaven but to be honest, I think I would prefer to spend eternity in hell.' St. Peter nods and the next thing the lawyer knows he's back in hell. But this time, there's smoke and fire and horrible smells, and men are being whipped by demons while pushing giant boulders. The lawyer frantically searches for Satan and when he finally finds him, he says, 'Satan, I was here only yesterday and everyone was playing golf and watching naked ladies and having a great time!' Satan strokes his chin and smiles and says to the lawyer, 'That was our summer associate program.'"

Hal got the joke since his mother worked at a big law firm, but Mike just looked at Seth with confusion. With a mouthful of Big Mac, Seth went on "Anyway, I'm Jewish, although apparently not too observant since I'm eating a Big Mac. We don't believe in heaven or hell. According to my dad, we suffer enough while we're living to make up for it." Mike, although raised Catholic like Hal, had gotten a bit into Buddhism through his girlfriend Eva. The subject of Eva was rarely trod upon, as, in Hal's opinion, she was one of those vegan know-it-alls who grated on Hal as soon as she opened her mouth. But since Mike was his best pal he largely stayed off the subject and bit his tongue when forced to spend time with the two of them. Mike thought that the Buddhists believed in reincarnation, and kind of liked that idea. Of course, Seth had to ruin the spirit of the conversation by saying he hoped he was reincarnated as Sofia Vergara's panties.

CHAPTER FIVE

Stephanie (Stevie) Raines was, from the earliest she could remember, more comfortable with horses than with people. She was painfully shy around both other kids her age and adults, and was happiest when alone with her horses. It was therefore fortuitous that she was born and raised in Lexington, Kentucky, home to some of the most beautiful horse farms in the country.

Stevie was seventeen and had dropped out of school when she was fourteen. She had little interest in studies, and her awkwardness made her the target of bullies both male and female. Stevie's mom had died giving birth to her, and while her dad Ben was a good man, he was also one to keep to himself, especially after his wife passed away. Ben managed a feed and grain store which provided adequately for him and Stevie. He was acquainted with many of the horsemen in the area because of his job, and was therefore able to take Stevie to the various farms and let her pet and feed the horses as a young child. When she was old enough, Ben taught her to ride.

From the first time she sat upon a horse, Stevie was hooked on horseback riding. When the horse would accelerate into a gallop, with the wind in her face and hair and holding on for dear life, she felt as if she was in another world, where nothing or no one could harm her. As she got older, several of the horsemen liked to bring her around to work with the more difficult or skittish horses, as she seemed to have an immediate calming effect upon those animals. Stevie counted the hours until school was out or the weekends would come so that she could spend all of her time around them. She and her dad had an unspoken agreement that while they would share meals together and be there to support one another when needed, they both preferred the solitude of their own company and pursuits.

After a particularly rough patch at school in her fourteenth year, she came home crying to her dad and told him she couldn't stand the prospect of going back. Her dad was torn by this, knowing that an education was important, but not wanting to see his child suffer from the cruelty of her classmates. Seeing as how she was so devoted to her work with the horses, he struck a deal with her: He would pull her out of school as long as she agreed to continue her studies at home with him. Ben knew he was no great shakes as a teacher, but he figured he could teach her enough math and other skills so that she would not be totally lost. He rationalized that she didn't need too much educating to be a groomer or trainer, and any additional education she needed she would get at the various farms.

Stevie was pretty in a plain way, with very straight wheat-colored hair that she wore in bangs, slightly large teeth for her mouth, but a winning grin and mischievous light blue eyes. Despite the rough time of it, she was a good kid, almost always cheerful, especially when away from school and with her horses. When she turned sixteen, Leroy Jenkins of Holyrood Farms offered her a full time job as a groomer which she accepted almost before he could get the words out of his mouth.

Mr. Jenkins was very fond of Stevie, both because he could see how much love she had for his horses, and because he believed she possessed a special grace that allowed her to turn even the most ornery colts into pussycats.

Stevie devoted more time to her grooming duties than was required, often arriving before six in the morning and refusing to leave until the sun had set. Holyrood had a large stable of racehorses, and Stevie would sometimes accompany Mr. Jenkins and his team to the various racetracks to keep the horses looking good and calm amongst all the noise and hoopla of the crowds. She was even invited on occasion to stand in the winner's circle with the winning horse and jockey while the fans (at least those with winning tickets) applauded.

Stevie was also an excellent rider, having spent as much time on a horse as her own two feet, and so she did not have too much difficulty convincing Mr. Jenkins to let her learn as an apprentice trainer alongside some of the trainers he used for his racehorses. Between all her duties, Stevie got to know many of the trainers and jockeys the farm favored, and for the most part got on well with all of them. The trainers and jockeys were unusual sorts, focused on stopwatches and hooves and splits, often smoking foul cigars and cursing up a storm. The fact that Stevie was a girl seemed to have zero impact on their behavior, which suited her just fine.

Her favorite trainer was Ed O'Neill, an ornery Irishman with a seemingly inexhaustible supply of curses and epitaphs, but underneath (way underneath) a heart of solid gold. He would take time out from berating the horse or jockey to give her tips on training, like how to tell if a horse liked to be a frontrunner or a closer, and how to adapt a training regimen to either style. He liked to remind her that these were beings just like humans, who had good days and bad ones, and sometimes were just not in the mood to run. He told her the most important thing for a horse to have was not speed or endurance, but intelligence. "A smart horse knows when to pace himself, when to stay out of a crowded lane, when to let another speed merchant burn itself out and then pounce, when to save ground and when to sacrifice it for an opening." When Stevie asked whether that wasn't the jockey's role, he replied "Sure, to some extent the jockey has to be smart too. Mostly he needs to know the horse he's riding and what that horse is capable of. But in the end it's all about the horse knowing what it needs to do to win the race."

The go-to jockey for Holyrood was undoubtedly Frankie Rodriguez. Frankie was in high demand due to his uncanny ability to get even the iffiest horses in the money, but his loyalties were with Mr. Jenkins, who gave him his start in the business and trusted him when he was still an unknown quantity. Jenkins treated Frankie like a son, and Frankie returned the favor, always looking upon him as the father he never had. Frankie was brought up in an orphanage in New Mexico, and had a tough time of it due to his size and sensitivity. He eventually made his way east and found a job as a stable boy at Holyrood. It soon became apparent that he had natural riding skills, and after an apprenticeship, he was given the occasional mount at some lower-level claiming races on horses which stood little chance of winning. But as Frankie continued to get more out of those horses than anyone thought possible, he was rewarded with better horses, and made the most of those opportunities.

Frankie and Stevie became fast friends, both of them sensitive and shy. They shared that rare trait of being able to communicate with horses without speaking, and even between each other words were often unnecessary, as they enjoyed the silences and their surroundings. She would give him insights on a horse she had spent time with, and in return he often took time out to sharpen her riding skills, demonstrating how a gentle tap of the whip would tell a mount to change direction or accelerate. He would joke about Stevie going professional, winning the Triple Crown and being on the cover of Sports Illustrated.

For her seventeenth birthday, Mr. Jenkins and Frankie presented Stevie with a custom saddle and a set of racing silks. The saddle, Stevie thought, must have cost a fortune, being of supple black leather with gold inlay, beautifully stitched and molded. The silks were pink and white and looked exactly like what the jockeys wore at the races, with a cap that had multiple pairs of goggles attached, so that when racing in the mud a jock could flip to a clean pair to see where he was going. Stevie couldn't wait to run home and tell her dad about these wondrous gifts. When she got there, he was in his familiar old green recliner with his glass of beer, and she gave him a big hug and told him about her new saddle and silks. He smiled and said "I can't compete with those gifts, but I didn't forget your birthday, Stevie." He got up and went to the bedroom, and when he came back he was holding a small wrapped box. Stevie unwrapped the box and when she looked inside there was a small gold pin in the shape of a horseshoe. Her dad, with tears welling in his eyes, said "I know it's not much, but it's the pin I gave your mom when we first started dating. I guess it didn't bring her much luck in the end, but maybe it will do better for you." Now Stevie was crying too and gave her father a fierce hug and a kiss and told him it was the best of all her gifts.

CHAPTER SIX

It was the night before the State track and field finals, and Hal was tossing and turning, unable to sleep. Exasperated, he got up and went downstairs to get a glass of milk and munch a few chocolate chip cookies. He was flipping through the latest issue of Sports Illustrated (his dad had gotten a subscription after Hal had gotten a one sentence "In the news" mention for breaking the state record in the 800) when he came upon an article about Frankie Rodriguez winning his one-thousandth race, and thought to himself he had a long way to go. Although his parents were not gamblers, they did on occasion take the kids to the racetrack as a semi-wholesome family day out, and his dad even put two dollar bets in for each of them and let them keep any winnings at the end of the day. Hal enjoyed the smells of beer and horse and hay and popcorn, and laughed at the histrionics of the bettors as they either rejoiced in or bemoaned their fates.

Hal trudged his way back to bed and somehow managed to get a few hours' sleep before his Homer Simpson alarm clock went off ("Go ahead, hit the little snooze button, you deserve a lie-in"). When he got downstairs, everybody was at the breakfast table, dressed and ready to go. Undoubtedly this was his mom's doing, making sure there were no stragglers for Hal's big day. Dad, with his inane and out of character man-speak: "So, champ, you ready to go out there and kick some ass?" Alison giving him a hug and wishing him luck, and even Petra managing to tear herself away from her iPhone for two seconds to smile and tell him to "rock their worlds." After managing to keep down a few strips of bacon and a piece of toast, Hal went back up to change into his running gear.

On the ride over to the meet, the inevitable subject of schools came up yet again. Hal had been offered scholarships at both USC and UCLA, and a partial at Stanford. Although it would entail more of a financial burden, his parents felt that Stanford was the no-brainer choice given its reputation for academic excellence. Hal was still leaning towards UCLA to be with Becca, but was being slowly worn down by his parents' logic about career and future. He knew he needed to make a decision soon as deadlines were approaching. He also knew that his parents would accept his decision and support him even if ultimately disappointed that he chose not to follow their advice. He short-circuited the discussion by telling them he wanted to get into his concentration for the meet.

The State finals were held at the university grounds, and Hal was a bit overwhelmed when he entered the stadium to see what looked like about ten thousand people in the stands. The participants' families had a special reserved spot, so he was able to find his family and exchange waves. The first race was the 800, Hal's specialty, and he won going away, not quite in record time but just a fraction of a second off. It was a comfortable win and as he looked over his dad was jumping up and down with fists pumping, and his mom was clapping wildly. Petra appeared to be texting someone.

The next race for Hal was the 400, and he knew it would be more competitive. The guy from King High was there again, the one who beat him last time. And there were a few other speed demons as well. As anticipated, the pace was extremely fast, and Hal was exerting himself to the max to stay in front. As they entered the final turn, it was clearly going to be between him and the King High kid. There was virtually no separation between the two of them as they headed for the line. From some heretofore unknown reserve, Hal found one more burst and leaned across the finish line a split second in front. The crowd erupted and Hal went down on the ground in total exhaustion. When he got up the kid from King High was waiting with hand extended, and as they shook the kid told him it was the first time anyone had ever beaten him.

Fortunately for Hal the 1500 was the last event of the day, so he had some desperately needed recovery time. He ate a banana and lay down for a bit, and gave himself a massage for his aching legs. Hal thought of the 1500 as the thinking man's race, where speed was almost a secondary factor.

It was all about pace, keeping close enough to the front runners without expending too much energy to find a closing kick. On the other hand, the closing kick wouldn't do you much good if you were too far behind. Hal remembered going to the races with his folks and watching the horse he had chosen go out to a huge lead, and jumping up and down in excitement, only to be crushed when the horse seemed to be running in quicksand down the stretch as every other horse in the field passed him. It must have made an impression on him, as he was always careful not to get too exuberant early in the race.

The gun went off for the 1500, and Hal settled in alongside a couple other runners, as two of the other competitors began to separate themselves from the field. At around the halfway point Hal was in sixth place, still comfortable but starting to worry that he was letting the frontrunners get too far ahead. At the 1200 meter mark Hal had improved to fourth, close to the second and third place runners but still far from the leader. As they entered the final lap, Hal thought it was probably over. He managed to get himself into second place, but there was still a sizeable gap between him and the leader. He still had some reserve in the tank and was beginning to make up ground as the leader began to weaken just a bit. As they ran down the final straightaway, Hal was eating up distance and it was going to be close. They approached the finish line and Hal had no idea who had won the race, it was that close. The stadium was going crazy, and when Hal looked at the board he saw that not only had he won, but had set a new state record for the 1500. His dad climbed out of the stands and ran over to grab him and swing him around as if he were three years old again.

That night, there was a big celebration. Dad sprang for dinner at Clancy's Steakhouse, one of those expensive places where the waiters were ninety years old and had matching demeanors. They all had embarrassingly large pieces of meat (except Petra, who opted for lobster) with heaping sides of string beans with almonds, mashed potatoes and French fries. Hal was even allowed a small glass of wine, although after tasting it was not sure it was such a treat after all. They finished off with crème brulee and cheesecake and fresh strawberries. Hal's dad faked a heart attack when the bill arrived, and everyone got a good laugh out of that.

The following Monday was the week before graduation, and Mike and Seth insisted on taking Hal out for victory pie after school. When they got to Vito's and went up to order, even the untouchable Jean congratulated Hal for his big win and leaned across the counter to give him a hug, which led to wiggled eyebrows from Seth and much needling at the table. Mike suggested that Stanford should now be on their hands and knees begging Hal to go there, and Seth sarcastically asked when his Wheaties box was coming out. Hal as usual took all of this in good humor, retorting to Seth that it would be the same time as his picture would be appearing on the Clearasil box.

Perhaps it was apropos or what writers call a "foreshadowing," that the last joke Hal would ever hear from Seth was about death. He had been talking about a torturous family trip last weekend to see his granddad, who was pretty far down the road with Alzheimer's. This got them on to the subject of how none of them wanted to ever live that way, which of course led to one of Seth's topical jokes: "I want to go like my uncle, peacefully in his sleep...not like the screaming passengers in his car."

CHAPTER SEVEN

On "The Fateful Day," as it was described ad nauseam thereafter, Sid Mackey was drowning his post-race sorrows at McKenna's Ale House, a somber Irish pub with an old mahogany bar and uncomfortable wooden stools. He was telling his woes to Mikey the bartender, who had long ago perfected the art of half listening. Mikey hated the afternoon shift, full of guys down on their luck who to boot were crappy tippers. Sid was one of the few he took pity on, having heard his life story over many sessions and having watched his own father destroy himself with gambling and drink. But even with Sid, the racing stories got monotonous. It was always "this close" or "just got nosed out of the trifecta" or "clearly interfered with." To Mikey's thinking, what losers like Sid or his dad never figured out was that losing was their destiny, and that whatever omnipresent being was having a good laugh at their expense was just teasing them to make them come back again and again for more punishment. The best line Mikey ever heard about gambling was that it was "the triumph of hope over experience."

Today's tale of woe was thus: "So it comes down to a photo for third. I got the first and second place finishers at 14-1 and 10-1, so if my horse gets third at 8-1, the tri is going to be at least a thousand bucks. So after about five minutes the board lights up and my horse comes in fourth. The horse that comes in third is also 8-1 and guess what the triple pays?" Mikey shakes his head. "Eighteen hundred and forty two friggin dollars! With a 6-5 chalk out of the money." Sid orders another low-end bourbon and recites for about the millionth time the gambler's mantra- "If I didn't have bad luck I'd have no luck at all."

While Sid was lamenting his cruel fate, Eddie and Nancy Porter were continuing an argument that had begun the night before. Eddie had finally summoned up the courage to ask Nancy whether she was happy. Sensing a trap, Nancy asked him what he meant by that. "It's a pretty straightforward question, hon. I'm asking if you are happy with your life?" Not wanting to have this conversation, she tried to deflect the question and move on to another subject, but Eddie persisted and so she finally said "I don't know Ed, is anybody really happy? I'm happy sometimes and other times I'm not. Do I seem unhappy to you?" returning Eddie's serve. Eddie replied "You don't seem very happy with me. I know we've had our issues and all that. I just wonder if it makes sense for us to stay together if we are making each other unhappy." This led to the predictable retort from Nancy "So *I* make *you* unhappy?" Eddie tried to defuse the tension, "Look, what I mean is that because I sense that you are unhappy it makes me uncomfortable and therefore unhappy. It's not that *you* are making *me* unhappy, it's that I think I'm making *you* unhappy."

Already deeply regretting his effort at marital honesty, Eddie was relieved when Nancy said she was taking a Valium and going to bed and that they would discuss it some other time. As it turned out, "some other time" was the next afternoon as they were driving to Home Depot to get some gardening supplies. Nancy started in with "If I make you so unhappy Eddie you should leave. All I've done is raise our two kids and deal with the house and every other fucking problem while you play around or go out with the boys." A voice deep in his subconscious was saying "Whoa, Man, *Let it go!*" but Eddie's temper got the better of him and he replied, "That's right, I just spend fifty or sixty hours *playing* at that goddamn job and heaven forbid when on rare occasion I try to actually enjoy myself, you treat me like some drunken lout who comes home and beats you. And *by the way,* it's not as if you don't find enough ways to piss all my money away at Nordstrom's and Macy's on your whims and impulses." This sent Nancy into a frenzy of counter-accusations which escalated the argument into a full-fledged screaming match.

At the height of said screaming match, Sid finished and paid for his last bourbon and shakily got off his stool. He left a dollar for Mikey. In the old days he was a good tipper, but the money was tight and every dollar left for a tip was one-sixth of a trifecta box bet. Between the booze and Sid's wandering mind, he failed to see the Porter's red Honda SUV as he jaywalked across the street.

As bad luck would have it, at the very same moment Mike, Hal and Seth were leaving Vito's to walk home. They had just entered the intersection when they heard squealing tires and looked up just in time...

In the middle of hectoring about some or other fault of Eddie's, Nancy suddenly screamed "LOOK OUT!!" as at the last second she saw a man directly in their path. Eddie was startled and turned the wheel to avoid the pedestrian, but then saw three kids crossing the street in the path he had swerved into. He slammed on the brakes, sending both of them violently forward, but not before he heard a sickening thud.

The world froze in varying ways for the participants. Sid was registering in his fogged brain how close he came to getting killed and wondered if it was a mercy or not that he hadn't. Mike looked at the SUV and the bug-eyed passengers within, without recognizing at first that Hal had been hit. Seth was having trouble breathing and grabbed onto Mike for support.

After this split second of inaction, everything happened fast, as if someone had initially pushed the pause button and then the fast-forward button on a remote control. Eddie and Nancy burst out of the SUV and came running over to where Hal lay. Nancy dialed 911 on her cell and screamed at them to come to the intersection of Plains and Morris streets, there had been an accident. Seth looked down at Hal, unconscious and with blood coming from the back of his head, and grabbed himself and began rocking and moaning. Mike went down to check Hal's pulse and breathing, and detecting neither, began to perform CPR. Sid just kept asking if the boy was okay, was he going to be alright.

The ambulance arrived a couple minutes later, and the attendants checked Hal's vitals and looked at each other grimly. They put Hal on a stretcher and hooked him up to an oxygen machine. With sirens blaring, they headed to St. Mary's Hospital.

Mike called the Carmody's home number but no one answered. He had no idea of Hal's parents' work numbers but managed to remember the name of Hal's mom's firm and got the number. After dealing with an officious receptionist, he managed to get through to Mrs. Carmody and told her about the accident. She asked a lot of questions about how Hal was, none of which Mike could or wanted to answer. Mrs. Carmody got ahold of her husband at the university, interrupting one of his classes, and they both raced over to the hospital, where Mike and Seth were already waiting. When they got there, one of the treating physicians told them that Hal was in the ER and they were doing everything possible for him.

The Carmody family had lived one of those tragedy-free existences where the worst things that happened were a lost phone or scrape on the new car or a zit coming out before a big date. So they were terribly unprepared to even think about losing a son or having him seriously injured. Mrs. Carmody finally got through to Petra and told her to get Alison and join them at the hospital, without going into the gravity of the situation.

For once, Seth was deathly silent, having no idea how to act in this type of setting. He sat with hands clasped and head down, just focusing on his breathing and saying a silent prayer that Hal was okay. Even Mike, the always composed one, was struggling with the situation, trying to assure the Carmodys that Hal was the toughest fighter he had ever known and that he would get through this. Alison had reverted to infant status, sitting on her dad's lap with eyes closed, just holding him for warmth and the comforting fatherly odors. Only Petra seemed pissed off by the situation, peppering Mike with questions about the driver, whether he was drunk, were the police involved, are they in jail, and so forth. Mike told her they did not seem drunk and that it all happened so fast he still was not sure what caused it.

After several hours of waiting in the drab, antiseptic room, listlessly skimming through the dog-eared magazines and watching the second hand on the large clock on the wall, a tall, youngish-looking doctor came into the room. Melody Carmody took one look at his face and burst into hysterical tears. The doctor knelt between Melody and Frank and said "I'm very sorry to tell you that your son did not make it. We tried to control the cerebral bleeding but the injuries were just too massive. I'm terribly sorry for your loss."

They all sat there in dumb silence. Even knowing that Hal had suffered a serious injury, no one in that room even remotely considered that he might die. It just did not happen. This was not real. It was out of a movie or mawkish after-school special. And in the movies the kid always recovered, with a sheepish grin saying something witty like "Next time I'll let Seth lead the way!" Frank was too numb and disbelieving to even cry, leaving the tears to the girls. For Mike and Seth, it was as if all the oxygen had been sucked out of the room and they were in some sort of trance.

CHAPTER EIGHT

At exactly 8:17 P.M. on October 4, the moment that Hal Carmody was pronounced dead, a foal was born at Holyrood Farms. The mare was named Caramancer, and she and her stud Fleet Admiral had been solid but unspectacular racehorses. But both came from good bloodstock and so there was hope that the first of their offspring might develop into a useful runner. Caramancer was a distance runner, specializing in mile to mile and a half races, while Fleet Admiral was a speed horse, preferring five or six furlong races.

Stevie was there to help supervise the birth, as she had been both groom and assistant trainer for Caramancer. Mr. Jenkins was there too, being hands-on about new foals born at the farm. While the messy post-birth tasks were being attended to, Jenkins pulled Stevie aside and said "I want you to name this horse and look after him and help train him. You have been a huge help to this farm and this is to let you know how much I appreciate everything you do around here. With the touch you have shown with these animals, I want to see what you can do with one of our babies." Stevie hugged Mr. Jenkins and told him she would make him proud, and he replied, "You've already done that, Stevie."

After everyone had gone for the night and the little foal was left in the barn with its mother, it woke up. Its first thought was "Where the hell am I?" and its second thought was "Man, it stinks in here! If I didn't know any better I'd think we moved into a barn!" Slowly adjusting to the dim light, Hal Carmody realized that was exactly where he was, which raised more questions than it answered. The last he remembered he was leaving Vito's Pizza with Mike and Seth. Everything else was pretty much a blank until he woke up here. The shock of waking up in a barn, however, was nothing compared to that when he looked down and saw he had four legs and a tail emerging from his backside. "Jesus Christ, I turned into a horse!" he thought. His next thought was just to relax, it was all a dream, like Bobby Ewing dying on Dallas, and he would wake up in his bed in Lincoln.

But by the next morning it became clear to Hal that it was not a dream, that he was in fact now a horse. He noticed the other horses in the barn, much larger than him, munching on hay. He was hungry, and went over to join them. After chewing on a mouthful, he spit it out and thought to himself "Yecch, this stuff is worse than those rice cakes mom used to buy to try and get us to eat healthy." He saw one of the other horses casually dropping several large turds and thought that at least going to the bathroom would be less involved, although he'd have to be careful where he stepped or lay his head down around here.

A girl around Hal's age entered the barn and came over to stroke his head. Hal thought to himself "this is more like it!" The girl said her name was Stevie, which struck Hal as strange since he always considered that a boy's name, but then thought about Fleetwood Mac and Stevie Nicks and it didn't seem so unusual. Stevie produced a carrot for Hal and he gratefully ate it up, as compared to the hay it was like a piece of pepperoni pizza! Hal thanked Stevie (at least in his head), and Stevie's eyes went wide. "Did you just say thanks?" she said, and Hal responded that yes, he had. Stevie shook her head from side to side and wondered for a moment if she was losing her mind. She knew the horse couldn't talk, since as a rule they did not, but she could swear that she was hearing the horse's thoughts.

Okay, she thought to herself, I know I have a way with horses but this is ridiculous! She said "Okay, Mr. Ed" (An old show she had watched as a child with her dad, about a talking horse and his hapless owner), "So what's your name?" The horse replied into Stevie's head "I'm Hal Carmody. Can you tell me how I got here?" Stevie wasn't sure what the horse meant, but said "You were born here." The horse replied that no, he was born in Lincoln, and this did not look like Lincoln. Stevie didn't know where Lincoln was, but she told the horse that "here" was Holyrood Farm in Lexington, Kentucky. Hal had never been to Kentucky and had no idea how he had gotten here, but those were secondary questions to the one he now asked Stevie: "Do you have any idea how I wound up in this horse's body? Last thing I remember I was having pizza with my friends Mike and Seth, and the next thing I knew I woke up as a horse!"

This totally floored Stevie, this horse talking like he was a boy out with his friends. She had no idea what to make of it. She started to respond that she didn't know how he got there when from behind came Ed O'Neill, who asked Stevie who she was talking to. "Oh, just the new baby, Ed" she shakily replied. Ed gave her a quizzical look and then went off to see one of the fillies he was training. Stevie admonished herself for holding a conversation with this horse, reckoning that there was probably not a lot of horseback riding privileges in the insane asylum. She told herself she was going to have to be extra careful with this one, and left the barn to ponder this mystery.

One of the countless ways in which Stevie did not fit into the world of her peers was her complete unfamiliarity with technology. This is not to say that she lived some sort of Amish existence. She knew how to drive a car and she watched television and had a CD player. But she had never owned a cell phone or a computer, didn't know what a "tablet" was (except in the biblical or pharmaceutical sense), and had never "surfed" the internet. When she read a book she held it in her hands. So she knew she was ill-equipped to tackle the mystery of this boy who claimed he inhabited the body of a horse. But even though the whole thing seemed completely crazy anyway, she thought she should try to look into it, if only to confirm she was hearing voices and seek proper medical care.

Mr. Jenkins' wife, Martha, volunteered at the local library, where Stevie sometimes borrowed books. Mrs. Jenkins was very sweet, an older woman but full of energy and always ready to help. She was admittedly surprised when Stevie came to her the next day to ask whether she could help Stevie do an internet search. "Why, I've never seen you take an interest in computers, dear. But as this is the twenty-first century, I suppose it's high time you learned how to use one!" She led Stevie to the library's computer room and sat her down in front of one of the PCs. After turning it on and starting

Internet Explorer, she asked Stevie what she wanted to research. Sheepishly, Stevie mumbled that she was trying to find out about a boy named Hal Carmony or Carmody or something like that. "Well, that's two surprises in one day," chortled Mrs. Jenkins, "First computers and now boys!" Stevie was mortified by this conversation, having no desire to discuss this topic with anyone, better yet Mrs. Jenkins. Sensing her discomfort, Mrs. Jenkins glossed over her comment and asked Stevie if there was anything else that would help the search. Stevie replied that she thought he was from somewhere called Lincoln. "Oh, dear," replied Mrs. Jenkins, "There are a lot of Lincolns out there!"

Mrs. Jenkins pulled up a website called "Google" which struck Stevie as hilarious for some reason. She explained to Stevie how to put in words or phrases to find information and then hit the little button with the magnifying glass on it. Mrs. Jenkins wished Stevie luck and told her she would be at the front desk if she needed any more help. Stevie thanked her and tried various permutations of Carmony and Karmody and Lincoln. When she used "Carmody" and "Lincoln" the Google thing said there were three hundred and eighty-seven matches, which struck Stevie as pretty overwhelming. After useless clicking on the first couple of links-- "Find Carmody Lincoln on WOW!" "Our Lowest Fares to Lincoln!" she found a link for a news article from a newspaper called the Lincoln Journal. She sucked in her breath as the article appeared on the screen:

"TRAGIC DEATH
OF TRACK STAR TEEN"
By James Albert
"Tragedy struck the close-knit community of Lincoln yesterday when local track phenom Hal Carmody was struck and killed by a vehicle driven by Edward Porter of Lincoln. The accident occurred near the intersection of Plains and Morris streets at around 3:45 pm, as Mr. Carmody and his friends were leaving a pizza parlor. According to eyewitnesses, the vehicle driven by Mr. Porter swerved to avoid another pedestrian and tragically careened into Mr. Carmody, knocking him to the pavement and causing catastrophic head injuries. Mr. Carmody was pronounced dead at 8:17 pm.
Mr. Carmody, seventeen, was the star of Lincoln High's track and field team, holding state records for the 800 and 1500 meters. He recently completed for the first time in

state history the 'trifecta,' winning the 400, 800 and 1500 meter races at the state finals. It was at that meet that he set a new record in the 1500 meters.

Mr. Carmody is survived by parents, Francis and Melody, and sisters, Alison and Petra. "

A myriad of emotions and thoughts were swirling through Stevie's mind. First, just plain sadness over such a senseless loss. The weird coincidence that Hal was the same age as Stevie. The weirder coincidence that he died on the same night that Caramancer gave birth to the foal. The fact that he was a runner. And of course, all this eclipsed by the fact that the horse back at Holyrood was claiming to be this boy.

Stevie didn't know much about religion other than what she picked up in dribs and drabs at school or on television. Her dad, as far as she knew, had never set foot in a church after the funeral for her mom. They rarely spoke about either topic, since there was not a lot to say, or, more correctly, not a lot of cheerful things to say. But her dad, after an uncharacteristic night of drinking a few years back, did say to her that after mom died he lost his faith in God. He didn't say it bitterly, just in a matter of fact way. Stevie wasn't too broken up over not going to church, as it would have cut into her time with the horses and created another awkward social occasion where she was bound to run into some of her schoolmates. And as far as she could tell, there was no greater evidence of a higher being than the green grass and majestic trees and the wind in her face when she was riding.

When she got back to the farm later that day, she decided to wait until it was dark and everyone was settled in before going out to the barn. She had stopped home on the way back and left a note for her dad that she would not be coming home for dinner as the new foal needed some looking after, which was not exactly a lie anyway. She busied herself with some grooming duties she had, and shared a meal with some of the stable boys.

When she was confident that the barn was deserted, she went back in and dragged a stool over to where the foal was sleeping. She gently nudged him with her toe and he opened one eye and then rolled to an upright position. Stevie took a minute to gather her thoughts and consider how to approach this discussion. Finally she said "This may seem like a strange question, but were you into track?" Telepathically, Hal responded (loudly in Stevie's head) "YES!" "Okay," said Stevie, "And are your parents named Francis and Melody?" The "Francis" threw Hal off for a second, as no one had ever called his dad by that name, but he realized that must have been his given name before everyone began calling him Frank. So again he responded in the affirmative. "Okay, last question: Do you have two sisters named Petra and Alison?" By this point Hal was a bit spooked that this stranger knew so much about his family, and so he asked her how she knew all this.

"I don't know how to tell you this other than to come right out and say it—you're dead. I went to the library and looked you up and it said that you had died in a car accident." Hal replied, "That's crazy, I don't even drive yet. I mean, I'm old enough, but I don't have a car yet." Stevie explained that as far as she understood from the article, Hal was walking when he was struck by an oncoming car. Hal was silent for a moment and then asked Stevie whether there was any mention of his friends Mike and Seth. Stevie replied that the article only mentioned Hal, so assumedly they were okay. "Look, I know this is a lot to take in, and I'm sorry to bring you such terrible news, but look on the bright side—at least you are getting a second chance. And there are worse things you could have come back as, like a worm or a fly or a snake. Anyway, is there anything I can do for you?" Although Hal was trying to absorb all of this, the one thing he did think of was food. "This hay is awful," he moaned, "Could you please bring me more of those carrots and maybe some apples?" Stevie laughed and told him she would, but warned him that in order to grow big and strong he was going to have to eat his oats and hay. She stroked his head for a minute and said goodnight, leaving Hal to his thoughts.

Hal was dizzy from everything he had just heard. Dead? He could only imagine how his family was suffering at this point, especially his mom and dad. Alison would be very sad but at least she had

Maya, and Petra would be sad for about a week before rediscovering the joys of her iPhone and her Facebook friends. But he knew his parents would have a hard time getting over it. Hal was their first child, and although they loved the girls equally, he had always had a special relationship with them. He wondered if there was any way to get a message to them that he was still alive and kicking, even if it was in the body of a horse.

He missed Mike and Seth too. It was strange to think that he would never see them again, never hear another of Seth's stupid but hilarious jokes. And although this girl Stevie seemed very nice, he wondered what he was going to do to keep himself from going crazy, with only horses for company. So far, their capacity for humor or gossip or anything approaching conversation appeared to be nil. They ate and shat and ate some more and that was about it. Finally he managed to drift back to sleep.

CHAPTER NINE

The funeral was held at St. Patrick's Church, and not surprisingly it was a full house. Besides all of the family and extended family and friends, Hal's track coach Mr. Beamon, was there, along with many of Hal's other teachers and Principal Frobisher. Even the kid he beat from King High showed up out of respect. The Porters had wanted to come but were counseled by friends that it might not be a good idea. Sid Mackey slipped into the church at the last minute and took a spot far in the back corner.

Reverend Green, who barely knew Hal, nevertheless did a yeoman job of listing his virtues along with the usual gibberish about how this was all part of God's plan, yada, yada, yada. After some prayers and hymns were sung, Mike was called up to the podium to say some words. The Carmodys had approached Mike about this, with Mrs. Carmody telling Mike that it was too emotional right now for her or Frank to trust themselves to speak, and asking Mike if he would be willing to say something at the funeral. Mike was both touched and terrified by this, as he had never been in front of a large audience before, except on a football field or baseball diamond. Even if he had wanted to, there was no way he could say no to Mrs. Carmody under the circumstances. So he stayed up that night trying to think of the right things to say. He was never at a loss for words when hanging out with Hal, but this was different, and he struggled mightily to come up with what to say to the mourners.

When he reached the podium, he looked out upon the sea of faces, many holding handkerchiefs to their eyes, and started to speak. "When Hal's parents asked me to speak about Hal to you today, I tried to compose something beautiful in his honor. But I guess that's not me, and I don't think it was Hal either. I think just about everybody that knew Hal liked him. He was funny, smart, talented, but never conceited or arrogant or mean. Everyone knows what a talented athlete Hal was, but I think he was most proud of being a good friend and a good son and brother. It was rare to hear Hal say a bad word about anyone, and maybe that's why you almost never heard anyone say a bad word about him. His generosity to me and his other friends was more than buying us pizza or movie tickets, it was his ability to listen and not judge, to have sympathy for the troubles of others, and to not shy away when things got tough.

As you all know, Hal loved to run. He told me once that there was a freedom from the world when he ran, that in those moments his sole concentration was on the rhythm of his legs and breath, the air on his face and the movement of his arms. That it was like he was in a cocoon, with nothing but the track in front of him. And maybe that's why he was so great, because nothing distracted or worried him.

I guess if I could speak for Hal today I would tell you that he would not want you grieving over him, or to remain sad or depressed. He would be pissed (sorry Reverend) at dying in such a stupid way, but he would find a way to laugh about it and move on, because that's the kind of guy he was. And I know he would want all of you to do the same. I'm not any wiser than the rest of you as to what happens to us, but knowing what a fighter and free spirit Hal was, and how he ran like the wind, I believe he is out there somewhere still smiling and running. We'll miss you, pal." And with that he blew a kiss to Hal and slowly walked away from the podium.

Hal's parents went to Mike and each of them gave him a long hug and a kiss, and thanked him for such a beautiful speech. Pretty much everyone in the church was crying. Becca was there with her parents and they were trying to console her, but she was wracked with uncontrollable sobbing, rocking back and forth.

After the ceremony and burial, the mourners gathered at the Carmody's house. There was a big spread of sandwiches and cakes, with coffee and soda. Mrs. Carmody told Alison and Petra they did not have to stay downstairs if they didn't want to, and the girls gratefully retreated to the solitude of their rooms. Seth continued to be in a near catatonic state, and Mrs. Carmody sought him out to embrace him and let him know what a good friend he was to Hal. Seth started crying and said "I wish it had been me. Hal was so talented and such a great guy. I thought when he became a big star he would dump a geek like me, but he always stuck by me. I miss him so much." Mrs. Carmody grabbed his chin and told him they all missed Hal, but that he would have wanted Seth to keep on telling his jokes and that somewhere Hal would be laughing along with him.

When everybody had finally left and it was just the two of them clearing up the mess, Melody turned to Frank and wondered how they were supposed to carry on. He said, "I feel like someone has punched me in the stomach and that it will never feel right again. And I don't know when, if ever, I will shake this feeling. We buried our son today, and there is no way our lives will ever be the same. But Hal would want us to carry on, and take care of his sisters and each other. We have two beautiful girls who need us and we can't afford the luxury of wallowing in our own misery. So we'll do what the Carmodys always do—keep our chins up and find a way to get through this."

CHAPTER TEN

Sid Mackey did not come to the Carmodys' home that day. He did not think that the man responsible for killing their son should accept their hospitality. Sid understood that technically the vehicle that struck Hal Carmody and caused him to fall and strike his head on the pavement was the event that caused the young man's death. But as Sid had learned from watching various legal dramas over the years, there was a concept in the law known as "intervening cause," which meant that something or someone in the chain of events could be responsible for an outcome. And Sid knew in his heart that if he had not stumbled out of that bar at that moment and carelessly jaywalked in front of that car, the boy would still be alive.

Sid returned to a recurring thought, namely that God had a wicked sense of humor. All of the worthwhile people around Sid—his wife June, this young kid—died, while God continued to let Sid live his meaningless existence, piling one layer of guilt on top of another. Sid had expected the police to come around at some point and question him about the accident, but apparently he was as invisible to them as he was to everyone else. The newspaper reports of the tragedy made no mention of an old drunk.

In an ironic twist, the lives of Eddie and Nancy Porter had in some respects taken a turn for the better. Although they were still devastated over the accident and the boy's death, and feared some criminal or civil consequences, their marriage had gone through a metamorphosis. Maybe it was the experience of going through such a traumatic event together. Or maybe it was the guilt they shared that a petty argument had led to a boy's death. Or maybe it was the starkness of the reminder that they were still blessed with two living boys. But whatever the reason, the fighting stopped and some of the passion returned to their lives. They were considerate to each other, and spent more time doing things together. And when one of them did something that annoyed the other, they bit their tongues and let it roll off their backs, reasoning that in the scheme of things it was unimportant. Anonymously, Eddie had started a scholarship fund at Lincoln High in Hal's name, and it had already raised over fifty thousand dollars.

In addition to the remarkable improvement in their marriage, Eddie and Nancy also became better parents to the boys, taking a greater interest in their schoolwork and activities, and planning more family outings. This was met by Sean and Marcus with somewhat mixed feelings, as while they were heartened at first by all the attention, they were frankly starting to get sick of it.

After a respectable amount of time had passed (and after the police and district attorney had determined there was no basis to press charges against the Porters), Eddie and Nancy phoned the Carmodys and asked Melody Carmody if they could come by. After conferring with Frank, she agreed to the visit. To say there was mutual discomfiture would be a vast understatement, but the Carmodys did their best to keep up a gracious front. Eventually Eddie Porter spoke. "Having two young boys ourselves, we can't begin to understand what type of pain the two of you are going through. If we could put ourselves in your son's place and bring him back to you we would do it in a heartbeat. We just wanted to come by in person and tell you how horribly sorry we are for your loss, and that you and your son are in our thoughts and prayers." Although Melody was a bit put off by the meaningless platitudes, she understood that it had taken courage to face the parents of the son you had killed, and so she was tempered in her response. "Thank you for coming and for your kind words. We understand that you never meant to hurt Hal. I'd be lying if I said I had forgiven you or didn't harbor resentment against you for what you did, but I hope in time those feelings will go away. If no other good comes out of this, I hope that you will treasure your boys and the time you have with them that much more."

Nancy Porter was stung by Melody's words, although she understood the lingering bitterness. When she finally spoke, in a tearful voice, she said

"I can hardly blame you for hating us, though probably not any more than we hate ourselves for what happened. And if it's any comfort, we relive that moment every day wondering what we could have done differently. If the old man hadn't been jaywalking, if we hadn't been momentarily distracted arguing about some meaningless slight. We hope that you find it in your hearts to forgive us. We understand if you can't."

With nothing more to say, the couples said their good-byes and the Porters got into their Volvo SUV (they had traded in the offending vehicle as they could not stand to look at it, not even haggling with the dealer over the trade-in value). The Carmodys watched them go and Melody, still the more bitter of the two, said she regretted having them over, that hearing their bullshit remorse did nothing for her, but only served as some undeserved absolution for them. A couple litigators at her firm had strongly urged her to sue the Porters for wrongful death, suggesting that a verdict in excess of a million dollars was well within the realm of possibility. But she ultimately decided against it. They really did not need the money, and a long, drawn-out civil suit would only serve as a constant reminder of their loss. So in the end she declined to seek any redress, and was relieved (albeit slightly disappointed from a vindictiveness standpoint) that the authorities had decided not to pursue criminal charges against the Porters.

Both Mike and Becca were occasional visitors to the Carmody home. Mike's decency and maturity constantly amazed Melody, as most kids Hal's age would have avoided his parents like the plague. But Mike came almost every week to see how they were doing and to reminisce about Hal. Although sometimes painful, on the whole it was therapeutic to remember the good times, and Mike had always been sort of a surrogate son to the family. For Becca, it was more to have someone to cry along with and to share her pain. She often spent hours up in Hal's room, just looking at his trophies and posters and geeky Marvel action figures, but mostly just taking in the lingering smells of Hal on his sheets and pillows and clothes.

Seth came by only once, accompanied by his mother, which spoke volumes about how anxious he was to be there. Melody knew that it was not out of lack of caring, but rather just the opposite, that Seth couldn't deal with the emotions and reminders of his best friend's death. And as Seth dealt with almost every situation by telling jokes, he was at a loss as to what to say to the Carmodys other than the perfunctory query about how they were holding up. Hal had been a big Stephen King fan growing up, and Seth returned to Mrs. Carmody a copy of Firestarter that Hal had lent him. Being a picked-on geek himself, he loved the idea of being able to spontaneously set fire to his tormentors. With Hal gone and Mike on his way to Duke, Seth felt more alone than ever, and was petrified of heading off to a new environment on his own. Melody joked with him that he would have enough to worry about not freezing his little tush off at Syracuse, and that the world loved people who could make them laugh. She told Seth not to forget the little people when he was a famous comedian.

The most overtly sad member of the Carmody family was Maya. She moped around most of the time, and spent a lot of time sleeping on or by Hal's bed. Often times she whimpered by his door, hoping he would magically reappear to take her for a walk and play with her. Alison also had a hard time and spent hours playing air hockey by herself down in the basement. Frank and Melody took the girls to see a psychologist, but it was clear after a couple sessions that the best thing for them was to get on with their lives and stay engaged in school and outside pursuits. They enrolled Alison in tap classes and she proved to be a bit of a prodigy, landing a role as one of the dancers in a local production of Yankee Doodle Dandy.

All in all, life returned to as much normalcy as could be hoped for under the circumstances. As Mike had so eloquently expressed at the funeral, the family tried to live up to Hal's wishes to carry on and be happy without him.

CHAPTER ELEVEN

Hal had begun to slowly adjust to life as a horse. He grew amazingly quickly, and was soon spending more and more time on the training grounds, learning the nuances between a trot and a gallop, and how to smoothly navigate the turns. There were still many things he had not adjusted to, however. He hated the whole horseshoeing process, and yearned for a comfortable pair (or pairs, as the case was) of Nikes. Despite Stevie's kindness in smuggling in lots of carrots and apples and the occasional sugar cube, he still struggled with the life-sapping bland fare of hay and oats. He lobbied Stevie for at least some milk, brown sugar and raisins for the oats, but only received a laugh and playful bop on the nose for his efforts.

Although he could not relate much to the other horses, he did try to be friendly and playful, and some of the horses responded in kind. Others were more surly, perhaps resentful of the special treatment he received from Stevie.

As for Stevie, she could barely wait to spend time with Hal, and she began to come earlier and stay later so as to finish her other duties and still have lots of time to spend with him. When it had come time to name him, Stevie chose the name Necromancer, based in part on his mother's name and in part on a book her mother than been reading before she died, about a girl with special powers due to government experiments on her mother and father, and the horse she loved. Hal was secretly thrilled with the name as he knew it came from one of his favorite Stephen King novels. But when they were alone Stevie always referred to him as Hal.

The bond between them grew stronger by the day. Hal was grateful both for Stevie's kindnesses and to have some human companionship. For her part, Stevie was fascinated to hear about the world outside Lexington, about Hal's travels, his girlfriend, his other friends and family. Never knowing anyone who had died besides her mother, who she never knew at all, she wanted to know about what it was like to die. Hal was sorry to disappoint her, but he had nothing to share, since he remembered nothing from the time he had been struck by the car until he woke up in the barn.

Hal was always happy to talk about track, about the freedom he felt when he was running, the thrill of the competition and the exhilaration of winning a race. He explained about the different strategies of the shorter sprints versus distance races, and how the races were as much about what your opponents did as what you did. Stevie told Hal that it sounded a lot like horseracing, as Ed O'Neill and Frankie had explained it to her. She asked Hal if it might like to race some day and Hal jokingly replied that if he couldn't get to the Olympics maybe he could settle for the Kentucky Derby.

When Hal was about a year old, Stevie cornered Ed O'Neill one morning and asked him to take a look at Necromancer. Ed had both affection for Stevie and a respect for her horse sense and so accompanied her to Necromancer's stall. What he saw was a fairly gaunt and gangly colt, hardly the second coming of War Admiral. He gave Stevie a skeptical eye and told her the horse looked more like a stray than a racehorse, but Stevie persisted. "I don't ask you for many favors, Mr. O'Neill, but I would be grateful if you would agree to train Necromancer. I know he's not much to look at, but he's super-smart and I think he knows how to run. Please just give him a try and if you tell me he's not going to be a racehorse, I'll accept your decision." O'Neill said he would discuss it with Mr. Jenkins, since he would be footing the bill for the training costs.

Later that day, Mr. Jenkins came to talk to Stevie about her discussion with Ed O'Neill. "Look, Stevie, you know I respect your horse sense and how wonderful you are around my horses. But this scrawny thing does not look like he'd last three furlongs. I need to devote Ed's time to horses that we think have a chance to win. But I'll tell you what. You continue to train this horse on your own, and if you can convince me otherwise, I'll reconsider after I see what he can do." Stevie was disappointed, but at the same time excited by the challenge of proving everyone wrong.

So Stevie devoted as much time as she could to training Necromancer. The truth was that it was the easiest time she had ever had training a horse, since she never before had the luxury of communicating directly with the horse. Plus, Necromancer already seemed to understand about pacing and strategy, knowledge learned from his track days. He never grew as big as most of the other horses, both because he remained stubbornly opposed to his imposed diet, and perhaps because of his prior human preference for the skin and bones look. But he was *fast.* Although she was not clocking his times, Stevie could tell just by the feel of riding him and the force of the wind in her face that he was probably the fastest horse she had ever ridden.

As the months went by, others at the farm also began to take notice of the little horse with the big engine. Other grooms and trainers began watching Necromancer's workouts and marveling at his acceleration. Finally one day Ed O'Neill showed up at one of his workouts and asked Stevie to push him for three furlongs. Ed stood by the rail with his cigar and his stopwatch and Stevie whispered to Necromancer to "knock their socks off." They took off and Necromancer galloped with intensity, gaining speed with every stride. When they reached the three furlong marker she slowly eased him down and they eventually trotted over to where O'Neill was standing, looking curiously at his stopwatch and seeming to shake it to see if it was working. Stevie asked, "So, how did he do?" O'Neill looked at her, then at the scrawny horse, then back at her. "Either my watch is broken or this pile of bones just ran three furlongs in 33:88. That's world class caliber for a three or four year old, better yet a horse barely eighteen months old. I'll talk to old man Jenkins about this. I want you to continue training him but I'm going to help out if he agrees."

Stevie's smile as she led Necromancer back to the barn threatened to tear her cheeks. She fed him extra carrots and apples she kept in a secret stash and told him how proud she was. Hal did not know how his time compared to what he would have run in the human world. All he knew was how good it felt to let loose and run with all his heart, just like a 400 meter race. And he was beginning to see the distinct speed advantage of having those extra two legs and a muscular backside. From then on, Ed O'Neill participated in Necromancer's training regimen whenever he was around, and he was dumbfounded how quickly the horse learned everything he imparted to it. He commented to Stevie that Necromancer was "one smart horse" and Stevie replied enigmatically "you have *no* idea."

While she loved being around Necromancer and having the types of conversations she was never able to manage with her peers, she remained troubled by a gnawing question. That question was what, if anything, she should do about Hal's family. On the one hand, she thought it might be best just to let sleeping dogs lie, as the family would have assumedly moved on from their grief and gotten on with their lives. Bringing up their son at this point might do no more than open up a world of hurt the family had managed to recover from. And of course the odds that they would believe that their son was alive and well and living as a horse in Lexington, Kentucky were remote.

On the other hand, she tried to put herself in the shoes of Hal's family. Wouldn't they want to know that their son was alive and happy, even in a non-human form? Wouldn't they want to visit him and touch him and maybe communicate with him the way Stevie could? While she could not make up her mind about what to do, she decided if nothing else she would try to find out where they lived so that she would be ready in case she decided to contact them.

She went back to the library to see Mrs. Jenkins, smiling and helpful as always. "So nice to see you again, Stevie! So what can I do for you?" Stevie explained that she wanted to try and find an address for someone. After explaining to Stevie about the different search engines (which Stevie thought was a strange term, since you didn't drive these things like a car or a tractor), Mrs. Jenkins took her back to the computer room and got her on the internet. "Go get 'em, Nancy Drew!" she laughed and patted Stevie on the shoulder. Stevie had no idea who Nancy Drew was but thanked Mrs. Jenkins and began searching for the Carmody's address. This proved more difficult than finding the story about Hal's death, and when she finally found a site that would search for addresses, they wanted a credit card payment. Stevie had never owned a credit card, but knew that her dad had one, as he sometime used it on the rare occasion they went out to dinner. Not wanting to explain yet to her dad about the whole Hal situation, and preferring not to lie to him, she asked Mrs. Jenkins if there was any way she could pay for it and Stevie would pay her back. Mrs. Jenkins hesitated, but sensing how much it meant to Stevie, ultimately agreed. After putting in her credit card details (first checking that the site was not dodgy), she left Stevie to conduct her search.

Stevie was amazed how quickly the site was able to find the family. And she was equally amazed by how much information besides the address was provided-like how much they paid for their house, where they had lived before, and so on. She wrote down the address, closed out of the site, and thanked Mrs. Jenkins, promising to stop by the next day and pay her back for the charge.

Armed now with the information necessary to contact the Carmodys, Stevie still struggled with what to do. She went to visit Hal in his stall and told him what she was thinking. It turned out that Hal was similarly conflicted, not wanting to reopen old wounds but thinking how cool it would be to let his family know he was still alive. "My folks are pretty open-minded people, but I seriously doubt they are *this* open-minded. But they would wonder why a girl from Kentucky would write to them about their son with such an outlandish story, so I can't say they would dismiss it out of hand. But I have an idea. Remember when I told you about my friend Mike?" Stevie nodded. "Mike's girlfriend was big into Buddhism and I think she was getting him into it as well." When Stevie asked what Buddhism was, Hal replied "I don't know much more than you about it, other than apparently they believe in reincarnation, that when we die we come back as something else. So maybe if you write to Mike he might be more inclined to believe it. At least it's worth a shot and it avoids directly confronting my parents with it." Stevie agreed that made sense and told Hal she would have to try and find his address, but Hal said that he remembered it and told her to get something to write with. As she fetched pen and paper, it dawned on Stevie how stupid she had been going through all the trouble to get the Carmody's address, as she could have just asked Hal. Oh well, she thought, I have more to learn as a detective than as a trainer.

When she got home from the day's work and after dinner with her dad, she went up to her room to go about the task of composing a letter to Mike Barber. Stevie was by no means dumb, but as her energies and interests were so focused on horses, she had rarely been called upon to write anything more complicated than a grocery list. So she struggled with everything after "Dear Mike." After countless pieces of crumpled up paper, about half of which she managed to sink in her trashcan, she finally came up with what she thought was the best she was going to be able to do:

"Dear Mike,

My Name is Stevie Raines. I live in Lexington, Kentucky. I work on a horse farm called Holyrood Farms. One of the horses I help train is called Necromancer. But his real name is Hal Carmody.

I know this will sound unbelievable to you but it is true. I looked it up and Necromancer was born on the same day that Hal died. I thought I was going crazy when the horse started talking to me with its mind, but I am certain that this is the same person that was your friend back in Lincoln.

I have spoken with Hal and he felt it was best that I write to you and you can then decide what if anything to tell Hal's parents. Hal trusts you and therefore so must I to do the right thing.

I can tell you that Hal is happy here and gets to run every day. He is fast and smart, just like the boy you remember. He told me to tell you he misses you and Seth very much and hopes you are both doing great.

Please write back to me and let me know whatever you decide.

Yours Sincerely,

Stevie Raines "

Stevie read the letter over several times, trying to figure out if there was anything else she should add, but finally decided to send it as is, and mailed it the next day to the address Hal had given her.

CHAPTER TWELVE

It had not dawned on Hal that Mike would have long ago gone off to college. Even if it had, Hal would not have known where Mike had ultimately chosen to go. So when Mrs. Barber received the letter with a Kentucky postmark she almost threw it away, thinking it to be junk mail. But she decided to put it aside. It was not until she spoke with Mike a couple weeks later that she remembered the letter, and asked Mike if he knew anyone in Kentucky. He said he did not think so, but asked her to post the letter to him anyway, just in case it was one of his school friends who had moved.

So it was that nearly a month had gone by before Mike received the letter. And, distracted by his classes and sports obligations and the occasional frat party, it was several days after that when he finally got around to opening it. His first reaction upon reading the letter was that it was a sick prank of the highest order, and he sat down with the intention of either just tearing it up or sending a sharply worded reply. But after reading it again, he began to wonder. Even if the prankster knew how to get his home address, how would they possibly know about Seth? And why would someone as far away as Kentucky even know about what had happened to Hal?

While the whole thing struck him as crazy, he had to admit that his curiosity was piqued. There was no way he was going to contact Hal's family without more to go on. So the first thing he did was call Seth. He had only spoken to Seth a few times since they both left for college, despite promises they would keep in close touch. Partly it was just the natural separation when friends go off to different colleges and gravitate to a new circle of friends. But although unspoken, there was also the aversion to places and people that reminded them of the loss of their good friend. Seth was surprised but thrilled to hear from Mike. Seth was struggling to adjust to college life, and Syracuse was bleak and miserably cold in the winter (and only marginally more tolerable in the fall and spring). Seth had a hard time making friends there, as the humor that had always seen him through in high school seemed largely lost upon the crowd there, who were more concerned with the latest music, fashion and political causes. So Seth managed as best he could, keeping himself entertained with movies, television and internet porn.

"Hey Mike, great to hear from you! So how's life down in tobacco country?" Mike raved about Duke for a while, and asked Seth how Syracuse was. Seth replied "Two words: Fucking Freezing!" He elaborated a bit on that, telling Mike the communications department was good and leaving out the loneliness and general gloominess of his college experience.

Mike said "Look, I know this is going to sound really weird, but I got this letter and I wanted to run it by you before I did anything." Mike went on to read the letter to Seth. There was silence on the other end of the line for a while, and Mike checked to see that Seth was still there. "Yeah, I'm here. Wow, that's some pretty fucked up shit. Have you told Hal's folks about it yet?" Mike said that he had not, and that it was one of the reasons he was calling Seth. "Well, this is definitely 'X-Files' territory. It's either a seriously sick joke, even by my loose standards, or there is something otherwise going on here. Have you looked up this Stevie Raines or the farm to see if they exist?" Mike indicated that he hadn't done anything yet other than call Seth. "Okay, I think we should investigate and see if this person and Holyrood Farm actually exist. If they do, then the next step would be to either write back to them or just go down there to see what's up." Mike told Seth this made sense and that they would talk further once he had found out more. After a few minutes of small talk about their families, they said goodbye and both immediately jumped on the internet.

Mike had no trouble finding a website for Holyrood Farms. Not only did it exist, but according to the site it was one of the largest horse farms in the country. There was a long list of decorated racehorses included on the site, as well as a large section on breeding services and fees. Under the "Contact Us" section of the site, there was an address provided and a toll-free number.

There was also reference to the availability of tours for those that were interested. There was no mention of Stevie Raines.

The next morning Mike called the number and asked for Stevie Raines. The receptionist asked what the nature of the call was, and Mike lied and said Stevie was an old friend. The receptionist asked for a number and told him that she would get a message to Stevie. Mike was not sure he wanted to give out his number, in case this was some sort of prank or scam, so he left a fake number with the receptionist. Afterwards he kicked himself, thinking that if Stevie was for real, he would never know, since he had left no way to contact him.

He Googled Lexington and saw that it was about four hundred and seventy miles from Durham, or about eight hours by car. His parents had given him their old Honda when he went off to college, so he could make the drive if he wanted. He called Seth and they compared notes on what they had found. Mike said that he was thinking of driving up to Holyrood Farms and Seth was adamant that he wanted to come along. "Anything to get out of Syracuse," Seth said, "Plus, if there's even a point one percent chance that this is real, I gotta be there!" Mike was secretly relieved that Seth wanted to join him as he was nervous about the visit whatever its outcome. So they agreed that Seth would fly down the following Friday and they would take the road trip together.

CHAPTER THIRTEEN

Stevie was concerned. It had been over a month since she sent the letter to Mike Barber. First there had been no response for a long time, and Stevie thought that either he never received the letter or, worse, he did get it and thought it was some kind of scam. Then, about a week ago, when she had gone up to the main house for some lemonade, Mr. Jenkins' secretary, Marilyn (who Stevie privately thought was a bit full of herself), stopped her and told her she had received a call from someone named Mike. After reminding Stevie that personal calls should be made and received at home and not at the farm (Ugh!), she handed Stevie a piece of folded paper with a number written on it. Rather than deal with the sure to be snotty response from Marilyn if she asked to use the phone, Stevie waited until she got home and dialed the number. To her disappointment, a recorded voice informed her that this was not a valid number. She wondered if Marilyn had taken the wrong number down out of spite. In any event, she was pretty much back where she started from.

Hal was equally disappointed when she told him the news. But he told her not to worry, that if it was not meant to be perhaps it was for the best, letting his friends and family carry on with their lives.

Hal's alter ego Necromancer continued to train impressively. Ed O'Neill had pushed the workouts at first to six furlongs, and was pleased with Necromancer's progress. And not even two years old yet, with growing still to do. When he pushed the regimen up to seven furlongs, the horse tired badly in the stretch, but O'Neill did not think this was due to lack of stamina but rather the horse's inexperience in pacing itself. He was proven right when in the last training session Necromancer fairly glided through seven furlongs in a very credible time.

While Stevie and O'Neill were busy training Necromancer, Mike was doing his best not to strangle Seth on the long (seemingly interminable to Mike) car ride from Durham to Lexington. They had already been forced to make three stops due to Seth's insistence on bringing a 128 ounce Big Gulp along for the journey, piling on the aggravation of the near constant burping and farting coming from Seth due to the ingestion of so much carbonated beverage along with an assortment of greasy snack foods. And of course Seth thought that every belch and stench bomb was funnier than the last. Mike was seriously tempted to abandon him at the latest rest stop. Seth did at least keep the journey interesting with his latest assortment of jokes, including a topical horse joke: "So the Lone Ranger gets captured by Indians and the Indian Chief says 'Lone Ranger, you are sworn enemy so we must kill you. But we have respect for you so we will grant you three wishes before you die. What is your first wish?' The Lone Ranger replies 'I want to talk to my horse Silver.' So the Chief nods and leads the horse over to the Lone Ranger. He whispers in the horse's ear and it goes running off. That night the horse comes back with a beautiful blonde on its back and she goes into the Lone Ranger's tent. The next morning the Chief says 'Lone Ranger, your horse have excellent taste in women. But you have only two wishes left.' The Lone Ranger uses his second wish to speak to Silver again. Silver goes bolting off and returns that night with an even more beautiful brunette, who goes in the Lone Ranger's tent. The next day the Chief says to the Lone Ranger 'Lone Ranger, your horse have unbelievable eye for women. But you are down to your last wish.' The Lone Ranger again asks to speak to Silver, but in the privacy of his tent. The Chief finds this strange but nods and the Lone Ranger leads Silver into the tent. He grabs Silver by the ears, puts his face right up to the horse's, and with an intense look says 'I SAID, BRING POSSE!'"

Along with Seth's jokes, the two of them passed the time discussing how they were going to try to figure out if this Stevie was crazy or leading them on or actually telling the truth. They threw out various ideas, none of them foolproof, and ultimately figured that they would just know when the time came. As Mike had called ahead and arranged for a tour of the farm, at least they knew they would not be turned away.

When they finally got to Holyrood, they were amazed by the size of it. A seemingly endless driveway led to the main entrance to the farm, where they were met at the security gate by a guard who look well past his sell-by date. He barely glanced at them before waving them through, and they found a spot to park the Honda.

The main house reminded Seth of one of those old slavery shows like Roots, or when his mom made him sit through the (seemingly) twelve hours of Gone With The Wind one night. He expected some old African-American to come shuffling out with a tray of iced tea. Instead, a smartly-dressed attractive woman was waiting inside the front door to greet them. Mike introduced himself and Seth and told her they were here for a tour. She checked her appointment book and circled an entry and said "Yes, I have you down. Please take a seat and I'll find someone to take you around." She indicated to a sofa that looked like it cost more than Mike's Honda, and they gingerly sat down upon it, with hands folded in laps like proper gentlemen.

A few minutes later, Marilyn returned with a kindly-looking older gent, tall and gaunt, who she introduced as Chet. "Chet has been here for nearly forty years and he knows every inch of this farm. I hope you enjoy the tour." With that, the two of them followed Chet out to an old, beat-up Ford truck. "Normally we like to take folks in a horse-driven carriage, as it's a bit more charming. So I hope you'll excuse the old truck. It's a bit hectic around here getting ready for breeding season and some big races coming up, so everybody's running around like chickens with their heads cut off. Anyway, we can cover more of the farm in this truck so you can get a feel for the place. So what brings you to Holyrood?" Mike answered "To be honest, Chet, we are looking for someone who we think works here, Stevie Raines." "Stevie!" Chet replied, "Sure, she works here. Has a real gift with the horses. She loves them and they love her back. So how do you know Stevie?" Before replying, it dawned on Mike that neither he nor Seth had considered whether Stevie was a man or a woman, and was glad he hadn't embarrassed himself by making the wrong assumption. He finally replied, "It's kind of a long story, but we were hoping you could take us to her." Chet said he'd be happy to and they drove off towards the stables. After getting out and making some inquiries, Chet got back in the truck and drove off towards the training track. When they arrived there, Chet pointed to a young woman in jeans and checkered shirt, wearing a racing helmet, who was putting one of the horses through its paces. "That's Stevie." He went over to the track and spoke to a man smoking a cigar and looking out through binoculars. The man made a signal to Stevie and she slowed the horse and dismounted. Chet went over to her and pointed at the two boys. Stevie took off her helmet and strode over to them.

"Hi, I'm Stevie, how can I help you?" Mike replied "Hi Stevie, I'm Mike Barber and this is my friend Seth. I think you wrote to me about a mutual friend of ours?" Stevie's eyes went wide and she exclaimed "You came! It had been so long I thought you didn't get my letter. Or you thought I was a nut job!" Mike smiled and said "Well, no offense, but I'll reserve judgment on the latter." Stevie laughed and told them to wait a minute. She told Ed O'Neill she was taking Necromancer back to the stables for some grooming, and beckoned for Mike and Seth to follow her. On the way to the stable she said in a low voice "Look, no one here knows about this. I'm afraid if they did they would send me to the loony bin, so we have to be very careful. If the coast is clear you can try to talk to Hal, who by the way is known to everyone else as Necromancer." They entered the stables and Stevie was relieved to see that they were empty except for the other horses.

She told Hal that his friends Mike and Seth were here, and Hal looked at the two of them, snorted and nodded his head several times. Seth tried to start a conversation "Hey Hal, you are looking even uglier than you used to! I didn't think that was possible." No response from Hal. Mike tried as well "Hey, buddy, ignore the doofus. He obviously hasn't changed one iota. So how is life as a horse?"

As he said this he felt like an idiot, talking to a horse. Again no response from Hal. Stevie asked "Are you hearing this?" and both Mike and Seth shook their heads in the negative. "Well, he is responding. It's just done through his mind. He told Seth something about 'the pot calling the kettle black' and Mike that 'the biggest downside is no pizza.'"

Mike asked "So how is it that you can hear him and no one else can?" Stevie just shrugged her shoulders and splayed out her hands. Seth said "So we have no way to tell whether this is Hal other than taking your word for it?" Stevie replied "Why would I lie? And why would I go to all the trouble of finding Mike if it wasn't true?" Seth had no ready answer for this. Mike said "Okay, I think I know how we can prove this one way or the other. I'll ask a few questions that only Hal would know the answer to. First, who is the goddess who used to serve us pizza?" Stevie responded "He says her name is Jean and that he is the only one she ever hugged." Mike was floored. "Okay, one more. What's Seth's nickname?" Stevie said "He says the main one is 'The Wild Man' but that others include 'Dork,' 'Geek' and 'Braceface.'" This sent Mike into a fit of laughter while Seth pretended to stew.

Mike said "Okay, I'm convinced. Wow, I can't believe it's you Hal! I wish we could sit down over a pizza like we used to but I guess we will have to make do under the circumstances with your interpreter." Stevie was keeping an eye out to make sure no one was around, and was getting nervous, so she suggested they take Necromancer for a walk on one of the trails so they could continue the discussion without being overheard.

There were lots of questions bandied back and forth, with Hal wanting to know how his family was doing and how Mike and Seth were doing at school. Mike related that he had seen the Carmodys over Christmas and that they seemed to be holding up okay, but obviously missed him. Seth bemoaned the endless winters up at Syracuse and the complete lack of sense of humor amongst the student body. Mike and Seth had lots of questions about life as a horse, and Hal, through Stevie, told them the ups (running, being outdoors, no school work, no worrying about leaving the toilet seat up) and the downs (the food, no Xbox, no movies or TV, the food). The sun was beginning to set by this time, and Mike realized they would have to get on the road soon for the long drive back to Durham, already planning a ban on any Mega Big Gulps for the return journey.

So he asked the only question that really mattered. "So what do you want us to tell your folks, or do you not want us to say anything?" Both Hal and Stevie were silent for a long time. Finally Stevie spoke up "Hal says that maybe it's best for now not to say anything. Since he can't communicate with you he's not sure he'll be able to communicate with them either, and he thinks it might be more upsetting than helpful to try this with them yet. He says he'll know when the time is right and he'll get me to get a message to you at that time. He asked me to tell you how grateful he is that you came all this way to see him and hopes that you'll come again sometime soon." Both Mike and Seth gave the horse awkward hugs and Stevie led them back to the stables.

They promised to visit again, and gave Stevie their cell numbers and addresses. Stevie gave Mike her home address and told him to write before they planned another visit so she would be ready for them. They said their goodbyes and thanked Stevie for looking after Hal. Although it was more than a mile back to the main house and parking lot, the boys said they were happy to walk back. With everything that had just happened, they walked silently with hands in their pockets.

The ride back to Durham was more pleasant, with Seth sleeping for much of the journey. Mike tried to distract himself with the radio, but all he seemed to be able to get were either country music stations or religious broadcasts, so after a while he turned it off and debated internally whether keeping Hal's family in the dark was the right thing to do.

CHAPTER FOURTEEN

Hal was energized by the visit of his friends and reconnection to his old world, and it showed in his workouts, which continued to get better and better. As Necromancer's second birthday approached, Ed O'Neill discussed with Leroy Jenkins racing the horse in the upcoming season. "Leroy, I'm telling you this horse might be something special. He's fast, maybe fast enough to win sprints, and he's learning how to pace himself at the distances. I haven't tested him beyond a mile, but based on his training runs I think he could get a mile and a quarter, maybe even a bit farther. Stevie's done a great job helping me and the horse obviously has an affinity for her. I think we should give Frankie a chance to ride him in an allowance race, somewhere low-profile, to see what he's got."

Jenkins responded "Ed, you know I trust your judgment. I've watched some of the horse's workouts and you are dead on regarding his speed. He's already right up there with some of our better six furlong horses. And he appears to be smart around the track, taking the right angles and saving ground. Frankie's riding down at Tampa so I'll enter him down there next month and we'll see how he does."

When Ed O'Neill told Stevie that they were going to run Necromancer in a race at Tampa Bay Downs, she was over the moon. "Wow, that's awesome! I know he'll do great!" O'Neill replied, "We'll, he's young and has never run competitively so don't get too excited. We'll see what he's got and go from there. But since you've put so much time in with the horse and he seems to be most comfortable around you, I'd like you to accompany me down to Florida." Stevie was thrilled to be invited to see Necromancer's first race and ran off to tell Hal all about it.

Hal was both excited and a little scared about being entered in a real race. He had always loved competing, but that had been as a human. He didn't know how he would fare with other bigger horses, and he knew that unlike human races, there were no defined lanes the horses ran in, and that they sometimes collided with each other or were injured taking a wrong step. He had marveled at his own physique, with its heavily muscled body supported by toothpick legs, and knew that, unlike humans, a broken leg on a horse could be a death sentence. Still, he was jazzed about the opportunity to compete again and outrun and outthink the other horses.

The first thing he found to hate about racing was the travel. He had never left the farm before, and when he saw the tiny trailer he would be riding in all the way to Florida, he was a bit freaked out about it, so it took a while for Stevie and the handlers to get him in there. The trip down was as nightmarish as he had envisioned, claustrophobic and bumpy and cramped. At least there was some air flowing through the slots on the sides of the trailer. By the time they arrived in Florida, he was pretty out of sorts, and Stevie could sense his discomfort as he was unloaded from his trailer.

When they got him settled into one of the stalls at the racetrack, Stevie stroked him and fed him a couple apples she had brought along. "I know you didn't much care for the trip, but now you're here and you can relax. Tomorrow's a big day so get lots of sleep and you will feel better by then. I have tons of faith in you so I know you'll go out and do great." She gave him a kiss on his nose and left him to rest up.

On the morning of the race, Stevie, O'Neill and Frankie visited Necromancer in his stall, and took him out for a morning run so that the horse could get familiar with the surface. Frankie had never been aboard the horse before and was impressed with the smooth acceleration he showed around the track. O'Neill also looked pleased with the workout and everyone was feeling pretty good about his chances.

He was entered in a six furlong allowance race for horses that had not previously won a race. There were two other first time runners, but the other five horses had previously run, with a couple of those having multiple starts and finishing second or third in prior races. Not surprisingly, those horses were the betting favorites in the race. As a complete unknown other than his posted training times, but from a barn with a good reputation for first-time starters, Necromancer's odds were a respectable 11-1. As the horses paraded around the track towards the starting gate, Hal looked over to see Stevie beaming and waving at him. He was reasonably calm cantering around the track, but as he was being loaded into the starting gate he felt like he had a bowling ball in his stomach. He was in the number five gate, with horses on either side of him, one of which was rearing up and almost threw his jockey off.

Hal knew from watching races that the bell would sound and the gates would open and that would be his cue to run. After the number four horse was calmed down and everyone resettled, the bell went off and the gates opened and they were off. Hal settled into his old racing routine and went right to the front, along with the number two horse. They stayed first and second through the first half of the race. As they approached the three-quarter mark, the number eight horse, one that had run previously and been in the money, made a big move and took over the lead.

Necromancer was still second at this point and Frankie went to his whip and began furiously whipping Necromancer's back flank to get him to keep up the pace.

In all his training runs at the farm, Hal had never tasted the whip, and so he was unprepared for what Frankie was doing to him. And he did NOT like it. It wasn't that it hurt all that much, it was more the indignity of it all, like he was some black cotton picker on a plantation who had displeased his master. So instead of picking up speed and challenging the leader, Necromancer all but stopped entirely and let the other horses pass him. He crossed the finish line last.

It was a somber mood back in the stable. O'Neill asked Frankie what had happened. "I don't know. The horse was going along fine and we were well-positioned, but when I asked him for more he had nothing in the tank. Maybe he burned himself out. It's only his first race so hopefully he'll get better at the game." When everyone else had left and Hal and Stevie were alone, she asked him what had happened. "He whipped me! There was no way I was going to stand for that!" Hal said excitedly. "I was running my heart out and this jerk rewarded me for that by beating on my backside with a stick!" Stevie stifled a laugh, seeing how angry Hal was at the moment. Finally she said "He wasn't trying to be mean, Hal. That's what jockeys do when they want their horses to run faster. It's my fault for not preparing you for that. I'm sorry." Hal told her she had nothing to be sorry for, that she was not the one beating on him.

Ed O'Neill called Leroy Jenkins back in Kentucky and they discussed the race. Jenkins said "Looks like he just gave up the ghost out there. What do you think?" O'Neill replied "It's just his first race. He looked great through four furlongs. Maybe he was just trying too hard and expended too much energy at the start. He was being pushed by the two horse. Let's give him another try, enter him in an allowance race down here in a couple weeks and then we can reevaluate." Jenkins agreed, and O'Neill spent the next two weeks working the horse out and getting him to pace himself over the six furlong distance.

A few days after the first race, Stevie approached Frankie and started up a conversation about Necromancer. She had been struggling to find a way to talk to Frankie about the whip without letting on that she and Hal could talk to each other. "Hey Frankie, got a minute?" Frankie replied that he always had time for Stevie. "Great. I know this might sound strange, and I know you are a great jockey. But I'm just wondering whether you might want to not use the whip with Necromancer? I was watching the race and it seemed like he didn't like it." Frankie laughed and said "Stevie, you are one of the nicest and best horse people I know. And you have a special bond with these horses. But this is racing. It's serious business, and a lot of time and money is invested in these racehorses. And it's my job to get them to the finish line in first place. I've ridden hundreds of horses, and I'm not saying they are dumb animals but they're not the smartest either. They need to know when it's time to kick it into another gear. And that's what the whip is for." Stevie said she understood and lamely added that perhaps he might consider holding back on using it in the next race. She desperately wanted to tell him about Hal, but although she liked and trusted Frankie, she couldn't bring herself to do it.

They had entered Necromancer in a five and a half furlong race, hoping that the shortened distance would help him stay throughout the race. There were only five other horses in the race which they also thought would help him stay focused and out of traffic. Before the race, Stevie came into the stall to give Hal a pep talk. "Okay, so this is your big chance! I know you are fast and you can eat these other horses for breakfast, so just go and do it! And don't worry about the whip. Frankie doesn't mean anything by it. It's just what jockeys do, so don't take it personally." Hal said he would try, and gave Stevie an affectionate nuzzle.

Having been through the routine, Hal was less nervous the second time around. Based on his last-place finish in the prior race, he went off as the longest shot in the race at 23-1. Hating the whip, Hal decided before the race that he would go out to the lead so that there would be no reason for Frankie to use it. As the bell sounded and the gate opened, Hal did exactly that, and opened up a decent lead on the other horses. He continued to maintain the lead and even widen it a bit, and was feeling great as he entered the final turn before the homestretch. He was therefore even more stunned when Frankie began to whip him again, from side to side. Furious, he stopped cold, sending Frankie flying over top of him onto the track. He heard a collective intake of breath from the crowd, as he watched the other horses and their jockeys swerve to avoid trampling Frankie.

It could have been much worse. Frankie sustained a separated shoulder and was taken off by ambulance. When they led Necromancer back to his stall, Ed O'Neill couldn't even bring himself to look at the horse. He had been embarrassed and proven a fool for thinking the horse had what it took to win races. Stevie was also furious with Hal, thinking that he could have killed Frankie. She wouldn't speak to him and left it to others to load him into the trailer for the long ride back to Lexington. Hal knew that he had overreacted and was sick with himself for causing the accident. If he thought the ride down to Florida was long, it was the blink of an eye compared to the ride back.

CHAPTER FIFTEEN

It was a lonely week for Hal upon returning to Holyrood. Other than being fed or led around for exercise, he had no contact with anyone other than his fellow stablemates, whose conversational skills were sorely lacking. Stevie did not come by the entire week, although he caught glances of her looking in from time to time.

Hal was angry with the world but most of all with himself. He had always been a pretty even-tempered sort which made it all the more inexplicable how he had completely lost it during the race. He thought part of it might have been that he had never been the target of injustice growing up, and so he had not been forced to react to it. And although he still felt that Frankie was partly to blame for whipping him, he knew that his reaction went way beyond what was right, and that it was only through sheer luck that he had not caused a catastrophic injury or even death through his actions.

Stevie remained very angry with Hal for days after their return to the farm. She was not only angry with Hal putting Frankie at great risk of serious injury, but upon the reflection his actions had on her, as she had been his biggest supporter. But what she was most angry about was the wasted potential, since she knew that Hal could have easily won that race but for his temper and immaturity. But deep down she still had affection for the horse and couldn't stay mad forever. After avoiding the stalls for over a week, she finally came to visit Hal, but without pockets filled with the usual treats.

Before he could say anything, Stevie asked "Why would you hurt all of us so badly when all we wanted was for you to be successful?" Hal closed his eyes and replied, "First of all, I am so sorry for what I did. Please let me know how Frankie is doing." Stevie told him that Frankie was recovering well from the fall and probably would be fully healed in a couple of months. "I'm relieved to hear that," Hal continued "Look, I have no excuse for acting like such an ass. I know you had explained about the whip, so I went out fast, thinking if I could lead wire to wire there would be no reason for him to use it. So when I had a good-sized lead and he still proceeded to use the whip I just freaked. I was so pissed I just decided to stop in protest, without even thinking of the consequences. I've been beating myself up ever since. I know I hurt not only Frankie, but the reputation of Mr. O'Neill and the farm. And most of all I hurt you, my best friend in the entire world."

Stevie was touched by this. "Listen, it's not the end of the world. Frankie will be okay and Mr. O'Neill has plenty of other horses to train. No one is talking about sending you to the glue factory." Hal laughed at that and said "But the thing is, I know I could win races for the farm. I promise I'll behave from now on if they'll just give me another chance." Stevie replied "I honestly don't know if that's possible. Mr. Jenkins is still pretty angry, and I overheard him and Mr. O'Neill saying that you did not have the temperament to be a racehorse. But let me see what I can do."

Stevie waited a few more days, scared to broach the subject with Mr. Jenkins. Finally she mustered up the courage and went over to talk with him. "Hi, Mr. Jenkins, how are you and Mrs. Jenkins doing?" Jenkins looked at her a bit sideways and replied "We're fine, Stevie, thanks for asking. So now that the pleasantries are out of the way, what is it that I can do for you?" Stevie, a bit embarrassed by her obviousness, hesitated for a moment before asking "I'd like you to consider giving Necromancer another chance. I know he screwed up really badly, and don't ask me how I know, but I just know that he will do better if you give him one more chance." Mr. Jenkins pursed his lips and remained silent with his hands folded behind his back, rocking on his heels. Finally he replied. "First off, that horse has cost us a lot of money with his antics. Second, he cost me my best jock for at least two months. Speaking of which, even if I were willing to give him another chance, there's no way Frankie is riding him even when he's healthy enough to ride again. Third, the horse either lacks the temperament or the smarts to win races. He stopped both times and that's not the sign of a winner. So, no, Stevie, I'm sorry, but I can't see my way to putting another jockey or the farm's reputation at risk."

Stevie looked directly into Mr. Jenkins' eyes and said "You know how hard I work around here and I never complain or ask for anything. I love it here and I'm grateful for the opportunity you gave me when my life was pretty sad. And I know you trust my judgment about horses. So if I have any favors to call in, I want to use them all to ask you to reconsider. Let me propose this: Give me a chance to run Necromancer over six furlongs here at the training track. If he can run fast enough to satisfy Mr. O'Neill, you'll give him one more chance, okay?"

Jenkins smiled at Stevie and said, "First of all, you have never raced a horse before. I know you have tons of riding experience but a flat out sprint is something different. So before I'd even consider it I would want to talk to your dad and get his approval. Even if I do, I don't think this horse has much of a chance to run fast enough to satisfy Ed after what he's done. But if your dad approves I'll give you and the horse one chance. But understand that I mean what I say. Any misbehavior by the horse, any slip ups, his racing career is over. Do we have a deal?" Stevie nodded enthusiastically, hugged Mr. Jenkins and ran off.

When she got home that night, she brought up the subject with her dad. Although he was naturally a bit nervous about his little girl racing one of these giant beasts, especially one that had already thrown his jockey, he knew before he even said anything there was no way he could deny her without crushing her spirit and creating a void between them. So he simply said "Hon, you are old enough to make these decisions for yourself. I'm your dad, and you are all I have left, so of course I'm worried about your safety. But I've never stopped you from doing what makes you happy and I'm not about to start now. So all I ask is that you be smart and careful, and for god's sake show 'em all how special you are!" Stevie gave her dad a hug and kiss, and not for the first time thought how lucky she was to have such a supportive father.

Ben Raines came down to Holyrood the next evening to meet with Leroy Jenkins. "Ben, very good to see you! How's the business going?" Raines replied "Oh, you know, just good enough to keep me one step from the bread lines." They both had a chuckle over this and Raines continued "Stevie has told me about this proposed race and I won't stand in her way. But between you and me, it does make me a bit nervous. Is this horse a menace?" Jenkins replied "I honestly don't know. The horse has always been fine here at the farm, and I know that he and Stevie have a special relationship. But Necromancer did act erratically down in Florida and injured one of my jockeys. So I can't make you any promises. You still willing to go along with this?" Ben chewed his lip and finally said "I don't see much choice in the matter. The house is lonely enough since the missus died and I don't think I could take the silent treatment from Stevie, so I'll just say my prayers and keep my fingers crossed."

Once she got the okay from Mr. Jenkins to do the test run, she immediately went to the barn to tell

Hal. "So, the good news is I got you one last chance to prove yourself. Tomorrow you are going to run six furlongs with me aboard. The bad news is that you have to run fast enough to satisfy Ed O'Neill or it's over. And if anything else happens it's over too. So I need you to behave and to run like your life depended on it." Hal told her he would not let her down and that he was more than grateful that she had put herself on the line for him. "I can't promise you how fast I will run but I will put everything I have into doing the very best I can." Stevie told him she couldn't ask for any more, gave him one of her secreted apples, and told him to get a good night's sleep.

The next day, everyone was gathered around the practice track: Leroy Jenkins, Ben Raines, Ed O'Neill and a number of other farm hands, groomers and trainers. Stevie climbed aboard Necromancer in her racing silks and cap. Major butterflies flapping around in her stomach. As they approached the starting line, she leaned down and whispered in Hal's ear "Let's kick some butt!" Hal nodded and snorted and got set for the gun to go off.

The starting pistol was fired by Jenkins and the race was on. Necromancer went flying through the opening quarter and then the opening half, and both Jenkins and O'Neill were privately thinking to themselves that the pace was suicidal and the horse would slow to a crawl coming down the stretch. O'Neill tried to signal with his hands to Stevie to slow down the pace, but she was in another world, holding on for dear life to this rocket ship posing as a horse. For his part, Hal was determined to keep moving fast even if he collapsed and died at the finish line. Given his rebirth, he had a crazy thought that if he did drop dead, perhaps God would be kind enough to bring him back as pizza dough that Jean would lovingly knead with her beautiful hands.

When they reached the final turn and headed for home, everyone was amazed that Necromancer was still moving at a rapid pace, with no sign of slowing down. He bore down for the final hundred yards and as they crossed the finish line, Stevie held up her whip like one of the winning jockeys she saw at the track.

Ed O'Neill clicked his stopwatch as they crossed the finish line. He did a double-take when he looked at the time. He practically ran over to Jenkins and thrust the stopwatch in his face. Jenkins' eyes went wide and then he conjured a smile just as wide. Neither Stevie nor Hal had any idea how fast he had run, but he knew he had done his best, and had managed not to drop dead on the track, although he was pretty winded. Stevie led Necromancer over to the rail and asked Mr. O'Neill how they had done. He put on a somber face and shook his head and said "I'm sorry, Stevie. He didn't run fast." Then his face burst into a totally uncharacteristic grin and he said "He ran like a rocket! Congratulations to you both. I guess Necromancer has a new jockey."

CHAPTER SIXTEEN

While Holyrood Farms was buzzing with excitement over Stevie's and Necromancer's performance, Sid Mackey was nearing another kind of homestretch. He had never really shaken the guilt over the boy's death, which only seemed to confirm to Sid what a poisonous human being he was. First he destroyed his beloved June, then himself, and finally the boy. And, he thought, he was even too pathetic to muster up the will or courage to end it all. Instead, he meandered along on cheap alcohol and keeping company with the other bums at Lincoln Raceway.

He had managed to keep his job at the MegaMart, not because of any feats of competence but mainly because the bar was set sufficiently low. He didn't steal or assault the customers, so he might have even gotten the Employee of the Month parking spot if he hadn't had to sell his car to keep his wagering habit ticking over. He was working mostly nights, which suited him fine. It left his days free to fritter away whatever money he managed to make, and kept him from having to sit home alone with Jim and Jack while thinking of June. Although, truth be told, the last time he had treated himself to any booze without a generic label was at the Christmas party hosted by the store manager.

The weight of his life and its disappointments had finally reached critical mass, and Sid had a plan. He suffered from a back injury which had degenerated over the years. His doctor, Martin Pine, was one of those physicians who had four pharmaceutical reps in his office for every patient. When you finally did get in to see him, he had all the bedside manner of a DMV attendant. His expression went from smiling lechery after one of the gorgeous reps left his office, to the resigned and harried look of actually having to deal with sick people. But his one saving grace was a quasi-criminal enthusiasm for handing out prescriptions. Michael Jackson's doctor had nothing on this guy. So Sid knew if he complained enough he could get a prescription for Oxys or some equivalent, which in sufficient quantities would provide the coward's way out he so desperately sought.

As Sid predicted, Dr. Pine vaguely listened to Sid's tale of unbearable pain, while no doubt contemplating his next pharma-paid junket to Aruba or Curacao. After the perfunctory sixty second checks of his heart and breathing, the doctor wrote him out a prescription for twenty OxyContin tabs, more than enough to send Sid into the afterlife on a cloud of numbness. Better than he deserved, he thought.

CHAPTER SEVENTEEN

The Keeneland meet was a much bigger deal than Tampa. Bigger crowds, much better horses, serious stakes races. And the beauty of it for Stevie and especially Hal was that it was right there in Lexington, only a short drive away from the farm. It was only the second day of the meet, and the weather had been very rainy the night before into the morning, leaving the track a mess. It was officially graded as "Muddy," which Ed O'Neill thought was an understatement. He was nervously pacing outside the stables. Not only was he bringing a horse who had stopped cold in his first two races, but one that had never, ever, run in the mud. Ed knew there were horses that were hopeless in the mud and others that loved to run in it. He just had to hope Necromancer fell into the latter category.

He had seriously considered withdrawing the horse, especially given that his jockey was a novice about to be thrown into the lion's den-a mucky, messy lion's den. He was concerned for her safety.

But Stevie was adamant that she and Necromancer would be fine. And since they were not running until the eighth race, there was a chance the track would dry out a bit. Sure enough, the sun did peek out from behind the clouds as the races got started, and as the day went on there had been some drying out of the surface. Still gunky, but better than it was that morning.

As Stevie and Hal were getting ready for their big day, Sid Mackey was doing the same hundreds of miles away. Figuring he had no one to leave his paltry possessions to, he brought the last four hundred and forty-one dollars he had on this earth to the track, putting aside the forty-one for some last day libations to toast his wife and his gone-to-shit life.

As per his usual custom, he had gotten up that morning and purchased a racing form, which contained the horses running at different tracks across the country. The best of those meets was at Keeneland, so Sid took some time to look through the entries. Through some cosmic coincidence Sid would never know about, his wife and Stevie's mother had shared a liking for the novels of Stephen King, including his book Firestarter. It was the book left on June's nightstand the night she died. Sid couldn't bring himself to throw it away, and on those long nights when he couldn't sleep he would sometimes open the book and read random passages. In his earlier days Sid was at least an occasional reader, but since June died he rarely picked up anything more literate than a racing form. Heaven forbid he should actually spend his precious booze and gambling money on a new book. So having read bits and pieces of Firestarter over the years, he was familiar with the name of the horse the girl Charlie loved so, Necromancer.

So he took it as some kind of sign from above when he saw the name of the horse running in the eighth at Keeneland. However, that sign blinked out quickly when Sid looked at the performance summary of the horse: Two last places finishes, including one "DNF" (Did Not Finish). And these were at Tampa, against inferior horses. Putting this horse in with the big boys at Keeneland was the equivalent of having a Pee-Wee football team play the New England Patriots. The morning line was 30-1 but Sid was willing to bet it would be way higher by race time.

As ironic timing would have it, Sid was having a good betting day on the last day of his life. He had won several races, so by the time the eighth race rolled around at Keeneland, he had amassed nearly a thousand bucks. Given the coincidence between June's book and the horse running in that race, Sid figured it was a fitting if somewhat blasphemous tribute to his late wife that he put the remaining money on the horse (minus enough for a premium bottle of hooch on the way home-if you are going to go out, do it with style!). He figured the horse had a snowball's chance in hell of winning, but that was fine since he didn't need the money anyway. He managed to spend every last dime betting every which way on Necromancer, other than the fifty he had stashed away to spend his last evening in the splendid company of Jamison or Remy.

As the horses for the eighth at Keeneland slowly made their way to the starting gate, Stevie was taking in the atmosphere of the track, the crowds, the smell of the dirt and adjoining turf course, the other horses and their jockeys, and the companion horses which helped keep the racers calm. There were nine other horses in the race, which was to be run at six furlongs. Of those ten, Necromancer was by a fair margin the longest shot on the board, currently at 66-1. There were two co-favorites, each going off at 5-2, who were older horses with proven speed and who had run in much better fields.

By the time they reached the starting gate, Stevie's heart felt like it was going to beat right out of her chest, and she closed her eyes and took some deep breaths to try and calm herself. Hal had seemed outwardly calm, but he too was a bundle of nerves, knowing how much this race meant to both of them. And while he had always been able to size up his competition when racing as a boy, he had no idea what to make of the other horses, other than that they looked a lot bigger and battle-scarred than he did.

Finally the gate got loaded and the bell sounded and the announcer signaled that they were off! Hal stumbled a bit out of the gate, still getting used to the slippery footing. At the halfway point of the race, he was sitting dead last, about ten lengths from the leaders. As Sid Mackey and Ed O'Neill watched from their prospective venues, they both thought at about the same time "Oh well."

But as sometimes happens in racing, mysterious forces took over. Without Stevie's urging, Hal went wide of the other horses and began picking them off one by one. Eighth. Then sixth. Up to fifth. In fourth. Battling for and taking over third. As the horses reached the far turn into the homestretch, there were only two horses in front of Necromancer. And he was moving like the mythical Pegasus. He took second halfway down the homestretch and came alongside the leader about thirty yards before the finish line. There was fight in the other horse as well, and as they crossed the line together there was barely a nostril between them. The crowd was going crazy and even Ed O'Neill was jumping up and down.

Back at Lincoln, Sid was about to make the ritual toss of his betting slips onto the floor, but when he looked up the horse was making this crazy move, blowing past horses like they were standing still. When he got into third place Sid began screaming and swearing like a sailor, urging the horse on. By the time they got to the finish line Sid was sweating and felt like he had run the race himself.

The photo finish sign lit up on the tote board. Sid couldn't tell who had won the race, but he mused it would be the perfect capper to his star-crossed life that he would be given this moment of ecstasy only to have it snatched away by the stewards. He couldn't even bear to look at the tote board, so certain was he that they would give it to the other horse. He was surrounded by other bettors watching the simulcast so he figured they would make the appropriate noises when the result was flashed. And as if on cue, a groan came from several of those bettors. But as Sid finally looked up, he realized those groans were coming from those who had bet on one of the favorites. He had to look three or four times at the tote board to be sure he was seeing it right, and then had to fish out and check his tickets to see if he had bet on the same horse. Necromancer had won.

At the same time Sid was trying to calculate how much money he might have won, Stevie was jumping off Necromancer and holding both fists in the air in a showing of absolute glee. The crowd loved it, seeing this little girl riding a prohibitive longshot to a completely improbable victory. Even those who were tearing up losing tickets had little smiles on their faces. When they got back to the winner's circle Ed O'Neill grabbed Stevie and swung her around, and then grabbed Necromancer by the ears and called him "you son of a bitch." He pulled out his cell phone and called Leroy Jenkins, who upon seeing who was calling, blurted out in an ear-piercing voice "DID THAT JUST HAPPEN?" They laughed, and when Jenkins congratulated O'Neill, Ed told him that it was all Stevie's doing, that she rode that horse like she'd been doing it for twenty years.

Stevie was blushing wildly after hearing that, both because she struggled with receiving compliments, but mainly because it wasn't true. Sure, she had managed not to fall off the horse as it veered four-wide and took off like something out of NASCAR. But really she was just along for the ride. Hal had done all the work, had seen what needed to be done and did it. Of course she could never explain that to anyone other than maybe her two confidants. So she simply basked in the unjustified glory and passed a few knowing glances back at Hal.

For his part, Hal was more relieved than anything. He had been a real klutz stumbling out of the gate, and it had seriously thrown off his running rhythm. It wasn't until he looked in front of him and saw the field running away that he went into full panic mode, figuring his best chance was to get outside and run like he was being chased by a rabid Rottweiler. He also knew he had been a bit lucky, that by missing the early pace battle he had not used up as much energy as the horses closer to the front. Still, it was thrilling to win another race, and he thought maybe someday he might be known as Lincoln High's only "two species" athlete.

When the prices finally came up, Sid just stood there gape-mouthed. With the two favorites running fourth and sixth, and the horses behind Necromancer coming in at 9-1 and 33-1, the prices were astronomical. When all of Sid's tickets went through the cashier's machine, the total was $163,476. The cashier looked up kind of sheepishly at Sid and half-jokingly asked him how he wanted that.

CHAPTER EIGHTEEN

There was a jubilant mood back at Holyrood for the conquering heroes. True, it was only a lower-level allowance race, and the farm had seen much greater glory from many of its horses. But the way in which Necromancer won was still the talk of the farm, and Necromancer became a bit of a celebrity amongst the staff there.

Stevie too was getting an uncomfortable amount of attention. She had been happier in her obscure existence, never feeling the pressure of how to act in social settings or to the receipt of compliments. She did her best to keep a smile glued to her face and thank those who had nice things to say about her, but secretly she just wanted to be left alone with her horses. Mr. Jenkins had even offered her the opportunity to ride some of his other horses in upcoming races, but Stevie demurred, thanking him for the confidence he had in her, but telling him that she was fine just riding Necromancer.

After Keeneland, she had written to Mike to tell him about the race, and got a letter back telling her that he and Seth had been able to watch the replay on something called YouTube and were blown away. He asked Stevie to let them know when Hal would be racing next, and Stevie did her best to remember to send Mike a note when races were scheduled.

Necromancer ran two more times at Keeneland over the spring and early summer, winning again at six furlongs and even more easily at seven furlongs. Ed O'Neill had discussed sending the horse to a place called Belmont Park in New York for a stakes race to be run at the distance of a mile. Leroy Jenkins had some reservations, concerned about how the travel might affect the horse, given the earlier fiascos in Florida. He was also concerned about running the horse at a distance he had never raced at, at a strange new track, against horses that were proven winners. But O'Neill was adamant that it was the right move. "Look, Leroy, I don't want to jinx it but I think we might just have a potentially great horse on our hands. He's fast, that's for sure. But he also seems to understand the game, and that's rare amongst horses. When we ran him at seven furlongs, he put himself in perfect stalking position and left plenty in the tank to eat up the other horses in the stretch. And the way he was going he could have easily gotten the extra furlong and more. But we are never going to know what we have here until we test him at different tracks against quality opposition."

Jenkins was ultimately persuaded by O'Neill to run Necromancer in the stakes race at Belmont. When Stevie told Hal about the big news, he was not as excited as she thought he would be. "I guess that means riding in a cramped trailer for hours on end?" was his first response. Stevie chided him "You big baby, quit whining about a little road trip. This is your chance to take on the big boys!" Hal acknowledged that he was excited to be running in a prestigious race against good competition, to see how far he had come in the horseracing world. He still dreaded the ride, but figured he didn't have much choice if he wanted to be a famous racehorse. Before the trip, he had several training sessions at the mile distance and O'Neill was satisfied that the horse would have no problem getting the distance.

In addition to the excitement of riding in a stakes race, Stevie was also excited to be going to New York. Other than the occasional trip to other tracks and a special trip to Disney World for her thirteenth birthday, Stevie had never been outside of Kentucky. She had seen lots of movies set in New York, and was enchanted by the towering skyscrapers, bright lights and sheer volume of humanity. Mr. O'Neill, who was born and raised in Brooklyn, promised to give her a tour of the city.

When Mike heard from Stevie about the race, he contacted Seth and proposed they meet in New York and go to the race, which was on a Saturday. Seth immediately agreed, excited about the opportunity to see Mike again. Seth was still struggling to make friends at Syracuse, and the more he felt rejected the more he had begun to build a protective shell around himself, essentially cutting himself off from the rest of the school other than to go to classes or an occasional sporting event.

The ride to New York was not as bad as Hal had anticipated, and he managed to sleep through a fair bit of it, so by the time they got to Belmont he was feeling reasonably okay. He struggled as usual to get used to the cramped and strange stall, but he knew there was nothing to be done about it. Stevie had been going on and on about how excited she was to see the famous NEW YORK CITY, and while Hal was happy and excited for her, it also hit him hard in an unanticipated way.

Since coming back as a horse, Hal had tried to focus on his new life and not dwell on his former one. He guessed his mind had a coping instinct, otherwise he would have gone mad thinking about all he was missing out on as a young man. And the routine around the farm, and especially his time with Stevie, had largely distracted him from those kinds of thoughts. But Stevie's enthusiasm for her city tour left him feeling depressed. He remembered the first time his parents had taken him to New York, going up the Empire State

Building, taking the Staten Island Ferry by the Statue of Liberty, having a Hulk-sized sandwich at the Stage Deli, and going up to the top of Rockefeller Center to see the panorama of the city lit up at night. It was like nothing he had experienced before and frankly made other places he visited afterwards look pathetic by comparison.

At first Stevie was a bit rattled being in the big city, with the masses of people on the sidewalks causing her to feel claustrophobic and a bit panicky. She was also not used to the fast pace and rudeness of people who after bumping into her not only failed to say "excuse me" but more often than not gave *her* a dirty look. Still, she was fascinated by the diversity of faces and languages. She had seen a few foreigners in Lexington, but by and large it was a pretty homogenous community, at least in the part she lived and worked in. Here, it seemed like the whole world had gathered in one city.

Some of the buildings, like the Empire State and the Chrysler, she recognized from movies she had seen. She was surprised at how large and diverse

Central Park was, and was fascinated by some of the strange looking buildings on either side of the park, like the Dakota and the Guggenheim Museum. They were a bit pressed for time, so she only got to see the Statue of Liberty from a distance, but it was still cool to be looking out at it from across the harbor. And, at Mr. O'Neill's insistence, they had hot dogs and potato knishes from a street vendor, washed down with a Dr. Brown's Cream Soda. She was undecided about the whole cream soda thing, but the knish was awesome!

Returning to Belmont the next morning, she excitedly told Hal about her day in the big city. Hal was jealous but heartened to see Stevie so excited about it. He told her to be sure to tell Mr. O'Neill to take her for a real New York pizza next time they went, and a pastrami on rye too, adding "but not before you plan on sitting on me!"

Belmont, like Keeneland, was a pretty racetrack, and bustling with large crowds. Having a few races under their belts, Hal and Stevie were more relaxed about the race itself, although Hal was still a bit nervous about going up against a different class of horses. When they were led out for the pre-race warm-up, Hal checked out the other horses. They did not look too different from the ones he had seen in Tampa and Keeneland, so that calmed him down somewhat. As they entered the starting gate, Stevie gave him the customary "butt-kicking" encouragement.

As the gates opened, Mike and Seth were sitting near the finish line. They had tried to get Hal's attention but he couldn't see them in the crowd. Being money-strapped college kids, they pooled together to get a twenty dollar win ticket on Necromancer. As the race progressed, Necromancer had settled around mid-pack, fifth out of the nine horses. At about the three-quarter mark, he started making his patented move around the other horses, and as he entered the homestretch he looked poised to overtake the two horses in front of him.

But just as Hal was motoring towards a gap between those horses, the horse to his right veered over, blocking his way and causing him to check up and lose his momentum. He wound up finishing third.

While one might have thought that his trainer would be pleased with an in-the-money finish in the horse's first stakes race, Ed O'Neill was in fact red-faced and furious, screaming about a foul and demanding a steward's inquiry. Although far less knowledgeable about horseracing, Mike and Seth were also yelling, in less decorous language, about the dirty play from the other horse.

A steward's inquiry sign flashed on the tote board, along with blinking lights next to the numbers for Hal's horse and the other horse. After reviewing the tape, the stewards determined that the other horse had illegally blocked Necromancer down the stretch and awarded Necromancer second place. As the winning horse was not involved in the incident, there was no further change to the order of finish. O'Neill was somewhat mollified by the second-place award, but still angry because he was pretty certain that his horse would have won the race if not for the interference.

When they got back to the stall, Stevie apologized to Mr. O'Neill. He flapped his hands at her and said "You got nothing to apologize for, kid. There was nothing you could have done. You rode a beautiful race and if not for that idiot jock on the three horse you would have won." Hal also felt bad about not winning the race, and he, like O'Neill, felt confident he could have taken both frontrunners if not for the incident. It all happened so fast and so unexpectedly that he didn't have time to react. Still, he replayed it in his mind many times over the following weeks, thinking of how he might have avoided the interference and still won.

Mike and Seth were disappointed with the result (and the loss of their precious twenty) but impressed with the way Hal ran. They tried to talk their way past security to see Hal and Stevie, but the muscle-bound gent outside the stable area made it clear that any such attempt would meet with physical distress. Mike made a mental note to ask Stevie if she could get passes for them next time.

CHAPTER NINETEEN

The other person who was disappointed with the outcome of the race was Sid Mackey. Yes, Sid was still very much alive. Going from four hundred dollars in the bank to a hundred and sixty thousand changes a man's perspective. But it was more than the money that changed Sid's mind. It was as if, in one fell swoop, God had gone from punishing him to lavishing him with great fortune. And although he would not have counted himself as a spiritual man (superstitious, yes; spiritual, no), he did start wondering more and more whether there was some greater purpose underpinning his improbable reversal of fortune.

So Sid slowly began to dig himself out from the years of accumulated guilt and self-abuse. Not all at once, mind you. Like any gambler that has a freakishly lucky day, Sid's first instinct was to see just how indestructible his gambling fortunes were. Three days in Vegas and nine grand poorer, he got back home bruised and battered, but more grounded for the experience. So he stopped gambling entirely for a few weeks, and had broken that streak solely to bet on his savior Necromancer.

Although the horse did not win the race, Sid still managed to make a bit of profit. And like Ed O'Neill, Sid was pretty sure the horse would have won a fair race.

In addition to tempering his gambling habits, Sid also began cleaning up the rest of his life. He still had the occasional drink, but with far more emphasis on the "occasional." And on those occasions when he did spend some quality time with Mikey the bartender, Mikey was far happier to see him, due both to the more upbeat nature of the conversation, as well as the vastly improved tips.

Sid was shocked at how much better he was feeling now that he was not perpetually gravitating towards his next drink. His energy level seemed to have quadrupled, and the time freed up from his schedule of self-destruction found him reading actual books again and re-engaging himself into the living world around him. He even decided to take on some volunteer work now that he had enough in the bank not to worry about finances for a while. He struggled to find something he would actually be good at helping people with, since there were not too many organizations devoted to handicapping horses or getting blotto for under ten dollars a day. Having served in the military, he finally decided to look into volunteering at a local VA hospital, and managed to get a position in the cafeteria, serving meals to injured veterans and their doctors and nurses.

All in all, he was happier than he had been since before June got sick, and, like Ebenezer Scrooge, although he felt his happiness was somehow undeserved he was nevertheless enjoying his newfound lease on life.

CHAPTER TWENTY

Despite the loss at Belmont, the feeling around Holyrood about Necromancer was more upbeat than ever. Ed O'Neill and Leroy Jenkins had several discussions about how to plan out the remainder of the racing year for Necromancer. And although Jenkins felt like the others that the horse might well have won the race but for the interference, he was still taken completely by surprise when O'Neill said "I think we need to prep this horse for a possible triple crown campaign as a three year old. Those were very good horses he was running against, better than your average stakes field, and he was better than those horses. And that's with only six races worth of experience. I say we run him in another stakes race here at Churchill and one up at Saratoga later this summer. If he continues to show progress, we get him a couple prep races prior to the Kentucky Derby next May." Jenkins stared at O'Neill for a long moment, and said "Ed, you know I have great respect for you, but I have to ask whether we are getting a little ahead of ourselves here? He's a fine horse but the triple crown, really?" O'Neill did not miss a beat "I told you before this horse has the speed and the smarts. And now I think he's got the stamina, too. Granted, there's a huge difference between a mile race and a mile and a quarter or mile and a half, but we won't know until we try. There's a mile and an eighth stakes race at Churchill in June and a mile and a quarter race at Saratoga in August. If he comes out of Churchill okay we run him at Saratoga. If he does well there, well, then, you can apologize for doubting me."

And so that was that. Necromancer began training at the longer distances. At first, partly due to still learning the energy conservation game, Hal tired near the finish of those training sessions, especially at the mile and a quarter. But he had the advantage of understanding what O'Neill was talking about, and so began to more strategically set a pace which allowed for more of a finishing kick. By the beginning of June he was starting to feel like he used to running the 1500, confident that he could stay close enough to his competition and eventually wear them down.

Despite the occasional melancholy about missing his former life as a human, Hal was generally upbeat about his new life. If nothing else, he felt blessed and fortunate that he was chosen to come back at all. And in the scheme of things, racehorse was pretty darn good compared to rat or snake or fly or a thousand other things he might have come back as. He thought the only things he would have rather come back as were either another human or maybe a dog, and then he laughed to himself remembering Seth's off-color reincarnation fantasy.

He was still struggling with the fact that his family was unaware of his existence, and the next time Stevie came by the stall, he brought the subject up. "Have you heard from Mike lately?" Stevie responded that they corresponded about Hal's progress and racing schedule, but there had been no mention of the Carmodys. Hal said "I've given this a lot of thought. I have no idea if they will believe Mike, but if anyone could convince them it was not a cruel joke it would be him. My mom and dad think the world of Mike. If by some miracle I do well enough in these next races and get a spot in the Derby, then I think he needs to tell them and get them to come. And if he needs you to convince them then I hope you are willing to help. After all, Holyrood won't want to send its newest star to the funny farm even if you might seem a bit out of your mind." Stevie replied that she was willing to do whatever Hal needed her to, and that if the tables were turned, she would want her dad to know that she was alive and well and doing something she loved.

As a way to put her toe in the water, she brought up the subject one day at the training track with Ed O'Neill. "Hey, do you think it's crazy to think that a horse could actually talk to you and understand what you are saying to it?" O'Neill gave her an inquisitive stare and responded, "Well, I don't know where that question is coming from, but let me tell you a story. About fifteen years ago, when you were still soiling your diapers, we had a horse here, Rowdy Rascal. Now Rowdy was not the fastest or biggest horse around, but he was one of the ones who used his racing sense to far outpace anyone's expectations. He won a lot of races he had no business winning. When I trained the horse and would be talking to the training rider or jockey about pacing or strategy, the horse's ears would prick up and he would nod after hearing the instructions, as if he understood every word I was saying. And if that wasn't strange enough, he would go out and follow those instructions to the letter when he raced. The jockeys would tell me similar stories about talking to the horse before the race and the horse uncannily following the script."

O'Neill paused at this point to gather his thoughts. "Now, I never had an outright conversation with the horse nor did he ever talk to me in any verbal sense. And if that's what you are talking about, then you might want to seek some professional help or at least have your dad take you in for a cat scan. But I do believe that some horses can instinctively understand what you are telling them.

Does that answer your question?" Stevie nodded and dropped the subject for the time being.

She recognized that because Hal could not verbally express his thoughts, any attempt to prove that he could communicate or was formerly human would take a giant leap of faith on the part of the listener she was trying to persuade. And even if they did not think she was off her nut, they might suspect that it was nothing more than a parlor trick, like those old psychics who used to prey on the bereaved by pretending they could speak with the dead.

Since there was little point dwelling on the problem for now, Stevie immersed herself in getting Hal ready for the next big race at Churchill. O'Neill had carefully balanced pushing Necromancer at the longer distances without burning him out physically. And Stevie too had started to better understand the rhythm of the longer races and how to gauge when she and the horse needed to make their move.

The day before the race, the three of them travelled to Churchill and got Necromancer settled in his stall. Stevie had been to Churchill a couple of times with her dad, and the history and grandeur of the place always made her feel as if she were entering some sort of church for horses. This was of course the home of probably the most famous race in the world, or for sure in the United States, and there were reminders everywhere of past Derby glory, from the vendors selling photographs of past winners to the gift shop selling mugs with every winner listed on them.

Although Hal had never been to Churchill before, he had watched enough Kentucky Derbies to understand the gravitas of the place. He knew it was an honor to be running here, especially in a stakes race.

On race day, Ed O'Neill came to visit Stevie, who was keeping Necromancer company before the race. "Okay Stevie, this is the big time. A stakes race at Churchill. It's the seventh race on the card so you and I have some time to see how the track is running and whether there is a bias." Stevie had been taught about the so-called "track bias," which largely came down to whether the track was favoring the speed horses or the closers, and whether there was an advantage being along the rail or further outside.

O'Neill continued. "The good news is that there are only seven horses including ours in the race. The bad news is that every horse but ours has already won a stakes race. And while our Beyers are competitive, they are still low compared to most of the other horses." In her continuing education, Stevie had been taught about "Beyers," which were named for some guy who came up with a way to measure a horse's speed beyond the mere official times. She didn't fully understand the system, and frankly didn't think a whole lot about it, figuring the horse was either going to run fast enough to win or he wasn't. But she had seen the bettors at the track furtively going over these figures as if they held some biblical significance as to who was going to win the race.

Before the sixth race, O'Neill reappeared and told Stevie that in his opinion the track was not significantly favoring either speed or closers. "In our race, I expect two or maybe three horses to battle for the lead. It's up to you, but I suggest you hold back about mid-pack, hopefully keeping within two to three lengths of the leaders, and make your move somewhere around the mile mark." Stevie nodded and thought that made sense, and Hal communicated to her that he was in agreement.

On their approach to the gate for the seventh race, Hal and Stevie took in the atmosphere of the track. Although it was not anything like Kentucky Derby day, Hal still felt a buzz in the crowd and again was a bit awed to be racing on these grounds. All the horses were well behaved entering the gate, and the race started without a hitch.

As O'Neill had predicted, two of the horses angled immediately for the lead, with a third just off their flanks. O'Neill was heartened to see the leaders go at very fast splits for the quarter and half mile, and by the three-quarter mile mark, he could already see the third place horse struggling to keep up. Necromancer was sitting comfortably in fourth, and had almost overtaken the third place horse by that point. O'Neill felt that the biggest danger at that point was the huge chestnut colt to the right of Necromancer, who had a big finishing kick.

Sure enough, as the horses rounded the final turn, Necromancer and the chestnut made their move, and soon had passed the early leaders in the homestretch. There was not a lot between the two, but the chestnut was gaining by a slight margin. Hal put everything he had into the final hundred yards, but it was not quite enough as he lost by a long head.

Although Hal and Stevie were again disappointed by the result, they were buoyed by the surprisingly upbeat banter of O'Neill after the race. "Great job, Stevie! You did everything I asked of you and so did Necromancer. We just got beat by a better horse today, and that happens. But you beat a lot of other very good horses today and you should be proud of that. This horse is still growing and still learning and although we have a lot of work to do, I feel excited about our prospects." This was about as animated as Stevie had ever seen Mr. O'Neill (other than when he was really angry about something), and his enthusiasm was infectious. So instead of a glum ride back Hal and Stevie were excited about the future.

CHAPTER TWENTY ONE

Sid Markey's remarkable metamorphosis continued. The less he drank and gambled the more of the world he rediscovered. Meals became more than mere fuel to counterbalance the booze. He had again begun to appreciate the unique tastes of a curry or a well-seasoned piece of fish. He took time to savor the meals and to notice his surroundings. And although he was still alone, he did not mind dining by himself, with a good book in hand. Of course he did sometimes yearn for companionship, and although he was no spring chicken, he still felt he could attract a woman under the right circumstances.

He had seen the ads on television for the different internet-based dating services. During his down days, he would have an internal laugh about the ad he would place:

"Drunk, degenerate gambler with no income or means of support seeks vivacious, wealthy sugar mama for late night blackout drinking and romantic trips to the track. No fatties."

Now that he had started to get his life together, he felt he should give dating a shot. He went to the local pharmacy after getting a haircut and had some photos taken. Like almost everyone else, he felt that photos rarely gave their subject a fair break, but he finally decided on one that was not quite as hideous as his driver's license or passport photo. He signed up to one of the sites and downloaded his photo along with the following ad:

"Single gentleman, 50's, still with hair and sense of humor. Seeking to share rebirth of his life with attractive woman, 40's to 50's, with a kind heart and sense of humor. Enjoys movies, sports, the beach and dining out. Experiences were meant to be shared so let's share them together."

That was about the hundredth draft of the ad and he was sick of thinking about it anymore so he went with that, even though it still seemed sort of sappy and clichéd to him. He checked back daily for the first week and was mildly disappointed that no responses had come in. But the following week he had two potential matches in his inbox. One of these he dismissed outright, as it contained a lot of religious references and notions of long-term commitment, and he envisioned a very long night with that one. But the other sounded intriguing: A woman in her late 40's, certainly cute enough for him, who enjoyed movies and comedy clubs and travel, and was looking for a friend to share good times.

Her name was Eleanor, and he responded to her note suggesting they meet for coffee. He had heard some of the single women at the MegaMart discussing online dating, and they were firm believers in the coffee approach, as it afforded a quick exit strategy should things turn boring or ugly. This made sense to Sid, plus a bit of the old money-watching part of him thought there was no sense wasting dinner money on someone you were never going to see again.

Eleanor responded that coffee would be great, and they met the following week at a Starbucks. By some miracle, they actually found an open table and Sid brought over a couple of coffees. After a few minutes of awkward chit-chat, they relaxed into conversation. Eleanor explained that her husband had died two years earlier in a skiing accident in Colorado. He had remained in a coma for several weeks until finally one day he passed over. She had not dated at all for a year after that, but feeling that she still had a lot of life to live, she finally rose from her torpor and started going out occasionally. She told a few dating horror stories that put Sid at ease, including one where the guy who had invited her out spent most of the dinner either picking his nose or readjusting his man parts. They had a genuine laugh over this and Sid promised to excuse himself if he had to do either.

For his part, Sid told her about June and the leukemia, and how his life had taken some pretty serious shots after that. He left out the parts about disappearing into the bottle and his gambling problems so as not to scare her off too quickly. But he couldn't resist telling her about the magical day at the track when Necromancer helped turn his life around. Her eyes went wide when he told her how much he had won that day, and he told her not to get too excited, that it had just brought him close to even on the lifetime. She laughed at that, and told him she used to ride horses when she was a girl, and thought they were beautiful animals. She hadn't been to a racetrack in many years but had family in Upstate New York who lived not far from Saratoga, which she said was a lovely area.

They carried on for another hour or so, and finally Eleanor said she needed to run for an appointment. Sid asked her if she would like to go out again, and she readily agreed to meet him for dinner the following week. After that the relationship began to blossom in earnest. Sid was taken with her easygoing nature and grace, and found her very attractive. Eleanor enjoyed Sid's jokes and stories, and although she was never going to mistake him for George Clooney, he was a pleasant looking man whose company she enjoyed. And she sensed something that had broken in him that he was desperately trying to fix, and admired his resilience. Besides, she always had a soft spot for wounded animals and people.

For both of them, there was that hesitant but strong urgency to move things forward, as if a second chance at life was not something to be dawdled on. So after a month or so of dinners and movies and cautious kissing, Sid broached the subject of taking a trip to Saratoga. He had never been there in person, although he had managed to donate to the local economy via the pari-mutuel windows. But he had seen how quaint the track was, like something out of the 1800's, with women in fancy hats holding umbrellas and families enjoying picnics on the grounds. Plus he hoped it would give Eleanor an opportunity to visit her family.

Eleanor asked for some time to think about it. After all, she barely knew Sid and this was a big step forward, travelling and staying together. It wasn't that she feared something awful would happen. She was a good enough judge of character to know he was harmless and sweet. It was instead the fear that a weekend together might ruin this pretty good thing they had going. And a related irrational fear that things would go wonderfully and suddenly she would find herself in the midst of a "serious" relationship. She ultimately decided to err on the side of throwing caution to the wind—life's too short and all that nonsense—and told Sid she thought it was a fun idea.

Sid made the arrangements, but not without first checking the racing schedule. Old habits die hard. He was thrilled to see that his newfound friend Necromancer was running in a big race at Saratoga, and so he made reservations for that weekend, ignoring the exorbitant cost of getting a room during racing season.

CHAPTER TWENTY TWO

The challenge, as Hal saw it, was similar to what he faced running the mile back when he was a human. The speed races were more about just running your behind off and hoping you were faster than the other guys. As the distance increased, so did the requirement for strategic thinking. Not burning yourself out too early in the race or letting yourself get too far behind the other runners. Having an internal clock for your splits, so that you went as fast as you could go for each segment without losing the ability to have a finishing kick in the closing stages.

As he tackled the preparation for the mile and a quarter race at Saratoga, Hal tried to employ the same disciplines. He had significant help from Mr. O'Neill, who was explaining the pace issues associated with the race. What you wanted to achieve at the quarter and half mile splits in a mile plus race was significantly different than, say, a six or seven furlong race. A murderous half-mile split would spoil even a great horse's chance of winning a mile and a quarter race. Stevie was also taking in these lessons, having even less experience than Hal in the racing game. But because Hal understood things no other horse could, her job was made much easier, and in truth her main job was just to stay aboard and give Hal the occasional word of encouragement.

In the meantime, Frankie Rodriguez had healed from his injuries and was back to competitive riding, which created a dilemma which engendered a great debate at Holyrood. After coming second in two graded stakes races, Necromancer had established himself as one of the stars in Holyrood's stables. And historically Frankie had been the go-to jockey for the farm's premier racehorses. Further complicating the issue was the bad experiences Frankie had on Necromancer, including getting thrown and injured.

For Frankie, there was yet a further concern. Stevie had always been a good friend to him, and he was pleased to see her doing so well riding Necromancer. Like any good jockey, he wanted to win races and the purses that went along with those wins. And stakes races were particularly lucrative from that end. But he did not want to be seen pushing Stevie out of the way after all she had done with the horse.

The main debate took place between Leroy Jenkins and Ed O'Neill. Like any owner and trainer, they had had their fair share of arguments over the years, but this one was right up there with the best. Jenkins was firmly of the view that Frankie should ride Necromancer at Saratoga. "Look, Ed, we both know he's one of the best jockeys in the country. He's won countless important races for this farm. There isn't another jock out there I would trust an important race to. And while it's been cute and fun to see our Stevie out there putting her heart into these races, the truth is she's at best an apprentice rider. If someone came to you and said 'here's your choice of jockeys,' could you possibly in your right mind consider picking Stevie over Frankie?"

Ed acknowledged what Jenkins was saying, but responded "Leroy, I can't logically dispute anything that you've said. And it goes without saying that I think the world of Frankie and his riding abilities. But here's what I've seen in the time I've spent training and racing this horse. The horse responded poorly both times Frankie rode him. The horse has a great bond with Stevie, and has ridden his guts out for Stevie every time she's been aboard him."

Before he could continue, Jenkins interjected. "But, Ed, those were Necromancer's first two races. Sure, he performed poorly with Frankie on board, but that was a green horse. Totally different situation now." Ed shook his head and said "I'm not so sure. It's true the horse was inexperienced when Frankie rode him. But I don't think that's what caused the poor results. We've had enough first and second time out winners to know that a horse does not have to be experienced to run well. There's another dynamic going on here. We all sometimes lose sight of the fact that these animals have feelings and emotions just like you and me. I couldn't tell you why, but for whatever reason Necromancer does not like being ridden by Frankie and loves being ridden by Stevie. So if you ask me who the better rider is, then hands-down it's Frankie. But if you ask me who the better rider is *for this horse,* then I'm telling you flat out it's Stevie."

The two went back and forth a while longer, and at one point Ed even offered to resign as trainer. Finally, Jenkins threw up his hands and said "Okay, Ed, you win. But here's my condition: If Necromancer does not win at Saratoga, we switch to Frankie and I don't want any further discussion about it. I like you and I like Stevie but I have a business to run here, and sentiment unfortunately has little place in business calculations."

Ed never told Stevie how close she was to losing her mount on Necromancer. He did talk to Frankie, however, to clear the air about the situation. To his surprise, Frankie seemed more relieved than upset. "I understand, Ed. And I know it would have broken Stevie's heart to lose the ride. She's done a great job with the horse. And maybe you're right, maybe the horse just doesn't like me. I thought that was limited to the ladies and the bettors, but…" They both laughed at this and Ed patted Frankie on the shoulder and thanked him for his understanding.

The next day Frankie went to visit Stevie in the barn where she was grooming Necromancer. He congratulated her on how well she had done, and she complimented him on looking fit and healthy after his recuperation. Having some inkling of what had gone on between Mr. O'Neill and Mr. Jenkins (gossip on a farm works pretty much the same way it does in an office), she said to Frankie "I'm going to let you in on a little secret, but first you have to promise not to tell a living soul. And you have to promise not to think I'm crazy." Frankie was intrigued and agreed to the first promise. As to the second, he said "I don't think you're crazy, Stevie. But I guess I don't know until you tell me." Stevie nodded that this was fair enough, and continued.

"I know what happened in your races on Necromancer. He didn't like that you used the whip on him. That I know that is not the crazy part. The crazy part is how I know. I know because Necromancer told me." She saw the concerned look on Frankie's face and continued "I know how crazy that sounds. When the horse first started talking to me shortly after it was born, I thought I was going crazy myself. But it's been happening ever since. The horse not only talks, but understands everything I or anyone else says to it."

Stevie purposefully left out the stuff about the horse formerly being a boy named Hal and all that, thinking that Frankie had quite enough to digest already. As it was, Frankie had a curious look on his face, as if he were trying to decide whether Stevie was playing a practical joke on him. Finally he smiled and said "Okay, Stevie, I'll bite. Hey, Necromancer, if you can hear me, nod your head three times." The look on Frankie's face was priceless as the horse looked directly at him and with great grandeur slowly nodded his head three times, and then, for good measure, stuck his tongue out.

CHAPTER TWENTY THREE

Sid and Eleanor were both nervous and excited about their first weekend away together. Sid was just hoping to not screw things up. After all the turmoil in his life, that was the best he could come up with. Not some impossibly romantic weekend or anything like that-just don't screw things up with this very nice lady. Eleanor was in more of a mind to just relax and have fun and see where things took them. She had not been away with a man since her husband died, and in fact had not been naked in front of another person besides her doctor in over a year. She was reasonably content with her body, figuring that for a forty-eight year old she was still holding it together pretty well. And she was experienced enough not to be overly intimidated by the notion of intimacy. But still.

Sid picked her up in the Chrysler he had bought not long after the big win on Necromancer. It was used, but ran well and was in good shape. The plan was to visit Eleanor's family on the Saturday and then go to the races on Sunday. Sid was able to find a flight to Albany, and from there they would rent a car for the drive up to Saratoga. They made small talk on the drive to the airport and on the flight, both still feeling out the situation and being careful not to make it into something bigger than it was.

After arriving in Saratoga and getting settled into their room (nice enough but not three-hundred dollars nice in Sid's humble opinion), they got back in the rental car and drove to Eleanor's parents' house, which was located between Saratoga and Lake George. Although nearing the wrong side of fifty, Sid felt like a seventeen year-old going to meet his girlfriend's parents for the first time, butterflies in his stomach. They were greeted at the front door by a handsome couple, somewhere in their seventies but still fit and youthful looking. Eleanor's mother Shirley hugged her daughter and welcomed Sid to their home. Her dad, Edgar (Big Ed to the boys at the VFW), stuck out his hand and offered a firm shake. After catching up about the goings-on in the community (who died, who divorced who, who made a horse's ass out of him or herself), the conversation shifted to how Sid and Eleanor met. This had been discussed beforehand, with Eleanor insistent that her parents not know they had met on a dating site. Sid was puzzled as to why this concerned her, but was happy to go along to keep the peace. So they told the story about the imaginary mutual friends who had introduced them. Edgar mildly grilled Sid about his background, and they hit common ground over military service. Edgar was impressed to hear of Sid's volunteer work at the VA. Over dinner, Sid retold the tale of Necromancer, and Shirley kept asking Edgar "Can you believe that!" until Edgar said that for the fifth and final time he could in fact believe it. Shirley insisted that Edgar give Eleanor twenty dollars to bet on the horse, despite Eleanor's insistence that she was old enough to pay for her own wagers.

When they got back to the hotel, Sid told her how much he had enjoyed meeting her folks, and he actually meant it. She was pleased about that as well as her perception that they felt the same way about Sid. Although she was a grown woman, it was still important to her that someone she was dating got along with her family. In her experience, it made life a *whole* lot easier. It also put Eleanor at ease for the rest of the evening, and when she and Sid undressed in front of each other for the first time, it inexplicably felt as if they had been doing it for years. Sid was both impressed with how good Eleanor looked naked and at the same time self-conscious about how flabby he must look. But Eleanor seemed content with what she saw and that helped put him at ease as well. They didn't have the neighbors ringing for hotel security, but they satisfied each other and even managed a morning encore.

As Sid and Eleanor were getting ready for the day at the track, Stevie was with Hal, getting him groomed for his big race and feeding him extra apples and carrots to fatten him up a bit after the journey north. They had prepared as well as possible for the race, and both were cautiously optimistic about their chances. Ed O'Neill came to visit them, and they were surprised to see that Mr. Jenkins was with him, as he rarely left the farm. They both asked Stevie how she and Necromancer were doing, and O'Neill gave them the usual scouting report. "I'm not going to sugarcoat it, this is by far the toughest race this horse will have ridden in. These are all first-rate horses and three of the five have won at this distance previously, so we can assume they will have no problem getting home. As it's only a six horse race, traffic should not be an issue, at least during the early stages. One of the horses, Rummikub, will want to set the pace. My hope is that one or two of the others will take the bait and set a fast pace, which will set things up for one of the closers, preferably our horse. Although every horse in the field is dangerous, Luck O' The Irish is the biggest threat, and he will be coming like a locomotive down the stretch. He's chased down and beaten a lot of good horses. So that puts us a little between a rock and a hard place. Stevie, it's up to you how you want to play it. My suggestion is to lie back from the speed but keep closer to the pace so you have a shot at holding off Irish. But like I said, it's pick your poison, so I trust you'll make the right judgment as the race unfolds."

After some more words of encouragement and wishes for good luck, O'Neill and Jenkins left Stevie and Hal alone. They both pondered what O'Neill had told them and Stevie finally said to Hal "Look, we both know you are the brains of this outfit. I'm just along for the ride, literally and figuratively. So figure this out and let's win this damn race so that I can keep riding you and you can have your family reunion at Churchill next year." Hal responded "Gee, thanks for the 'no pressure' speech, Stevie. All I have to do is beat a bunch of wonder horses at a distance I've only ever practiced at the farm!" Stevie smiled and told Hal to "quit yer whining," and fed him another apple.

As Necromancer and the other horses were led out for the eighth race, Sid pointed to the horse and Eleanor gave him a skeptical look. "He looks like a high school guard going up against an NBA team," noting how small the horse looked compared to the others. Sid quipped "Size isn't everything dear" and Eleanor quipped back "You should know!"

Whether it was because of his size, or more likely his limited resume, Necromancer was by far the longest shot in the race, going off at 18-1. Luck O' The Irish was the 7-5 favorite, and none of the others were higher than 9-1. Sid placed bets for himself and Eleanor, and gave her the twenty dollar win ticket on Necromancer. Eleanor asked, "So if by some miracle this runt wins the race, what will I win?" Sid replied, "If the odds hold, you'll get back about three hundred and eighty dollars." To which Eleanor raised her fists in the air and shouted "GO NECROMANCER!" eliciting a few curious stares from the stands.

Hal felt a bit like a pig in a beauty contest as he headed for the starting gate, for some bizarre reason thinking of that hilarious scene from Spinal Tap where the midgets were in danger of trampling Stonehenge. Stevie gave Hal some final words of encouragement and they were off. As O'Neill predicted, Rummikub jetted out for the early lead. None of the other horses were biting...except Necromancer. The two horses were going stride for stride at a blistering pace, and if she had looked over, Stevie would have seen Ed O'Neill with his face buried in his hands and shaking his head from side to side. As far as O'Neill was concerned, this was the worst possible scenario, certain to lead to an embarrassing loss. He had already resigned himself to apologizing to Leroy Jenkins about making the wrong jockey choice. Sid was a bit calmer than Ed O'Neill, but was telling Eleanor that this was looking very ugly. When Eleanor questioned why it was a bad thing that their horse was winning, Sid replied "Because he's going way too fast for this long a race and he'll never keep it up."

By the three-quarter mile point, even Rummikub had backed off into second, and Necromancer was three lengths clear of the field. Predictably, as they made their way into the final quarter mile, two of the other horses, Minnie's Pearl and Luck O' The Irish, were eating up the rest of the field. Halfway down the homestretch, Necromancer's lead had been cut to a half-length, with Minnie on the inside and Irish on the outside. It looked over for all intents and purposes, with the only question being whether Necromancer could somehow hold on for third place.

But then a funny thing happened. Necromancer looked left and right and then seemed to nod his head, and somehow found a reserve he had absolutely no right to have. He picked up the pace, leaving Minnie struggling to keep up. Irish was still coming, a relentless mass of muscle determined to take his rightful place across the finish line. But Necromancer would not give way, and as they crossed the finish line he had won the race by a short head. The crowd was raucous, and Sid and Eleanor were hugging each other. It was by many accounts one of the greatest races ever run at Saratoga. The time was very close to the track record.

Ed O'Neill was not among those celebrating. He was too stunned to do anything for about a minute. He just could not comprehend how the horse could go wire to wire against that field. He was so resigned to losing, and losing badly, that it took Leroy Jenkins shaking him and hitting him with his program to finally snap Ed out of his daze. "That was INCREDIBLE!" roared Jenkins. Ed finally managed to smile and responded "I'll be damned. I was one hundred percent certain we had lost that race. The kid's either a genius or has a guardian angel somewhere. Well Leroy, barring an injury or some bad luck, looks like you got yourself a Derby horse."

Stevie was basking in the cheers and holding her whip aloft like she saw the other big jocks do. Inside, she was just as stunned as everyone else, asking herself what the hell had just happened. She couldn't believe it when Hal took off after the frontrunner, and even tried once or twice to rein him in. But finally she just figured he was going to do what he was going to do and just hung on. Her internal clock told her they were going way too fast to last, and she had braced herself for the inevitable collapse as the field passed her by. But somehow Hal had found the grit to hang on.

After the ceremony at the winner's circle, and the proffered congratulations, Stevie finally got a private moment with Hal and asked him what the heck he had been thinking. "Well, when I looked at how strong those other horses were, especially Luck O' The Irish, I honestly didn't think I could outrun them down the stretch. So I thought my only chance of winning was to get a big lead and pray I could hold them off. I hoped that Rummikub would fade at some point and that I could maybe get a breather. But before I knew it I could feel the big boys stampeding up my rear end. But then I guess I just got sort of angry and thought 'the hell with this, if I'm going down they are going to have to take it from me,' and I just gritted my teeth and ran as hard as I could. I was as shocked as anybody when I crossed the finish line ahead of Irish."

Sid and Eleanor celebrated their good fortune at a seafood restaurant near the racetrack. Eleanor went on and on about how exciting the race had been and how she now understood why Sid liked the horses so much. Sid, like most gamblers, had regaled Eleanor with stories about his big wins while leaving out the many, many, many days of losses and accompanying disappointment. Still, her enthusiasm was infectious, and it had been one of the most exciting races Sid had ever witnessed, certainly in person. So Sid sat back and surveyed his remarkable good fortune and not for the first time wondered what he had done to deserve it.

CHAPTER TWENTY FOUR

For the first time in as long as he could remember, Sid had something to do for the holidays besides drawing his blinds and drinking himself to sleep. It was actually kind of exciting shopping again for someone, and he went at it with gusto. He understood the convenience of online shopping, but was of the opinion it could not shine a light to getting bundled up in the cold weather and walking the streets, looking in decorated store windows and having the perfect gift jump out at him. The only problem was that it had been so long since he had shopped for a woman that he was basically clueless as to what she might want. He knew Eleanor dressed tastefully but not extravagantly, and wore the occasional bracelet or necklace, but nothing ostentatious. He picked up a few small gifts he thought she might like. As he passed one of the jewelry stores, he saw in the window a gold horse pin adorned with diamonds and emeralds, and went in to enquire about the price. When he was told how much it was, it reinforced the notion that he had not been shopping in a *long* time. He calculated how much of his existing stash this purchase would decimate, wandered around the store debating with himself, and finally thought "screw it," and told the clerk to wrap it up for him. Other than a house and car, it was by far the most money he had ever spent on a single item.

Eleanor, although a decidedly more veteran shopper, was facing similar struggles. Sid was clearly not the bespoke suit and aftershave kind of guy, and in fact did not seem to be partial to much by way of consumer goods. So she wracked her brain and finally had an epiphany. She ran back to her apartment, went online and found exactly what she was looking for.

At Holyrood, the annual Christmas party was festive as always, and Stevie and her dad were enjoying the plentiful food and good music. Although Stevie in theory had to watch her weight as a jockey, she was blessed with a hyper metabolism that pretty much let her eat as much junk as she wanted. Frankie was there too, and he had not forgotten about their last conversation. He pulled her aside and said "Merry Christmas, Stevie! So, I see the little wonder horse can do more than talk, huh?" Stevie smiled and gave Frankie a hug and whispered "Ixnay on the talking horse stuff, comprende?" Frankie laughed and theatrically drew a zipper across his lips.

Being reminded of Hal, Stevie excused herself, but not before raiding the fruit section of the buffet and collecting a large bowl of sliced apples. She went out to the barn and found Hal in his stall. She thought he would be thrilled to see a pile of his favorite food, but he seemed despondent. She asked him what the matter was, and he replied "It's hard for me, especially this time of year. I have so many great memories of family Christmases, and to think I'll never share another one with mom and dad and Alison and Petra is still tough to handle. I'd trade all my wins for one more Christmas with them." Stevie felt bad for Hal but there was not a whole lot she could do. Finally, she grabbed him by his head and looked in his eyes and said "If all goes well and we get to the Derby next year, I promise you I'll find a way to get your family there and let them know you are alive and well." She kissed him on the nose and left him the bowl of apples.

Back at the Carmody homestead, there was a similar feeling about the holidays. Joy that they were all together and healthy, but a glaring gap at the living room table when they sat down for their holiday meal. It had become a tradition after Hal died that they raised a toast to him before eating, champagne for Frank and Melody, grape juice for Alison and Petra (mortified). Then each of them would go around telling a funny or proud memory about Hal. It didn't make them miss him any less, but it felt right to keep him close in their thoughts and memories.

As coincidence would have it, Petra, as part of a senior-year project, was volunteering at the local VA hospital where Sid also worked. She would read to the sight-impaired soldiers, spend time with other disabled vets, and perform various chores as needed. At first she was pretty freaked out by the scene there, with the terrible sights of those soldiers who had been maimed or lost limbs. But as time went on she got more used to those sights, and felt real satisfaction from helping these men and women, who looked forward to her visits and were grateful for the time she spent with them. Petra had mixed emotions about the hospital. She was firmly in the anti-war camp, and her feelings were reinforced by seeing first-hand all the misery war brought with it. At the same time, she was in awe of the sacrifice these people had made for their country, and wondered what it must feel like to give yourself to a cause like that.

Sid and Eleanor had a Christmas meal at Eleanor's apartment. Although they had begun spending a lot of time together, they still maintained separate apartments so as not to put undue pressure on the relationship. Eleanor was no master chef, but knew her way well enough around a kitchen to prepare a turkey and some sides, which they enjoyed with a nice bottle of wine. After dessert and coffee, they sat by the apartment-sized prefab Christmas tree and exchanged gifts in ascending order of significance. When Eleanor opened Sid's big present, she gasped and brought her hand to her mouth, just like in one of those jewelry ads Sid saw on TV. "Oh, Sid, it's beautiful! But it must have cost a king's ransom! It's too much." Sid reached over and took her hand and said "The only important thing is that you like it. It's a drop in the ocean compared to what you have done for me. So wear it in good health and may it bring you only good luck." Eleanor had tears in her eyes and gave Sid and big hug and a long kiss and said "Be careful, mister. You keep saying things like that and you won't be able to get rid of me."

Eleanor handed Sid an envelope, and Sid joked that it must be his walking papers. He tore open the envelope and pulled out a sheet of paper that read:

DEAR SID,

ON MAY 3RD OF NEXT YEAR, PACK YOUR BAGS...BECAUSE YOU ARE GOING TO THE...

KENTUCKY DERBY!!!!

YOUR FLIGHT, HOTEL AND BOX SEATS AWAIT YOU!

LOVE,

ELEANOR

Sid was thrilled. He had never been to the big race, although he and June had talked about it once or twice. It was definitely one of the things on his "bucket list," and he was as excited as a seven year-old opening the hot toy for that year. "Eleanor, this is by far the most perfect present anyone has ever gotten me. I can't believe you thought of it!" Eleanor beamed and said "I had no idea what to get you, Sid. You seem to live a pretty spartan existence judging by your apartment. And then it hit me like a lightning bolt-what better gift to give a man who loves the races than a chance to see the biggest race of them all in person! Now all I need is one of those fancy ladies' hats to show off!"

After celebrating New Years' Eve at a local restaurant, where they had a serviceable band playing old hits and the requisite Auld Lang Syne at midnight, Sid and Eleanor took a taxi back to her place. Although he drank more than he had since the bad old days, his practice still held him in relatively good stead, so he did not stumble when he went down on one soon to be arthritic knee and asked Eleanor to be his wife. Eleanor, who was not nearly as well-versed in the art of alcohol consumption, giggled and told Sid to stop clowning around. Sid looked her in the eyes and told her he was serious. "I know what I want and that is you, Eleanor. Lord knows I've done enough lousy things in my life not to deserve you, but I can't help myself. You mean everything to me and I want to start building a life together. And please don't make me do this again because I'm not sure I could make it down on this knee a second time."

Eleanor realized he was serious, and began laughing and crying at the same time, partly because she was drunk but mainly from the emotion of the moment. When she composed herself, she said, "Wow, Sid, you sure know how to start off the New Year with a bang! I don't care about anything you might have done. I only know that you have been wonderful to me and for me since the day we met. So yes, I would be proud to be Mrs. Mackey. Just promise me things won't ever change between us."

CHAPTER TWENTY FIVE

Although Necromancer did not race for the rest of the year, Ed O'Neill had kept him on a steady training regimen, and the horse continued to run well and stay fit. As the New Year ticked over, he began to strategize about getting the horse ready for the Derby. A horse had to accumulate a certain number of points based on performance at key races in order to qualify for a spot in the Derby. O'Neill had been fortunate enough to train three other horses that had qualified for the Derby, but his best finish in the race was fifth. He thought that Necromancer was better than the other horses he had sent to Churchill, but he reckoned that he had probably thought the same thing about those other horses before they ran in the Derby.

Still, he felt he had learned a lot from his prior experiences: Not giving the horse too many starts during the two year old campaign. Not using unfamiliar jockeys on the horse when he could avoid it. Not leaving the horse too lightly raced going into the Derby, making sure he was battle-tested. Making sure the horse was in one or two races with large fields, so that he would be comfortable running in a race with twenty horses such as the Derby. Of course, all of that and a few bucks would get you a cup of coffee, as the updated saying goes, unless everything clicks at just the right couple of moments in May.

For his part, Hal had gotten over the holiday blues and was pretty much back to his old self. He was anxious to get back out and race, but understood that there were reasons for the time off, both to keep him fresh and to avoid possible injuries. Still, it was a bit monotonous going through the same training regimen again and again. If not for Stevie's daily visits he thought he might have lost his mind just hanging around the barn day after day.

After Saratoga, Stevie had been approached both by Mr. Jenkins and by some other outfits to ride other horses, but she politely declined, telling everyone that she had a monogamous relationship with Necromancer, which never failed to get a laugh. She did toy with the idea from time to time.

After all, she was not completely immune to the accolades and celebrity that came with winning a big race. But those thoughts never turned serious, since she was happiest just working at the farm and spending time with Hal.

The other project she began to busy herself with was how to get Hal's family to know about his situation. She had finally broken down last Christmas and accepted the gift of a cell phone from Mr. Jenkins, who insisted he might need to get in touch with his famous jockey in case of an emergency, ha, ha. Although she still failed to see how this annoying little device, with its bleeps and blings and shrill rings managed to enthrall her peers, she had to admit it was useful for keeping in touch with Mike. They had been speaking regularly, figuring out the best way to approach this highly unusual task.

A decision had been made by O'Neill and Jenkins that they would race Necromancer three times in preparation for the Derby, and in order to get the necessary qualifying points. The first race would be in February at the Fountain of Youth at Gulfstream at a mile and a sixteenth. Then the Rebel at Oaklawn in March, also at a mile and a sixteenth. Finally, the Blue Grass at Keeneland in April, at a mile and an eighth. Stevie and Mike agreed that if Necromancer did well in the first two races, he would make the dreaded visit to the Carmodys in late March so that there would be sufficient time to make plans to get them to Churchill, assuming he was not escorted out of their house in a straightjacket.

Mike and Seth had also kept in close touch to discuss the problem, and had bandied about several possible approaches, none of which was greeted by great enthusiasm. Of course, Seth could be counted upon to come up with the ultimate in politically incorrect approaches, such as dressing us as a horse, and accompanied by eerie music, announcing that he was their long lost son Hal. The biggest question in Mike's mind was whether they should go together since, to his credit, Seth was prepared to do whatever he could to help, and a second witness was not necessarily a bad thing. On the other hand...there was Seth.

Not necessarily the guy you want when you are pleading with a cop or a firing squad. Mike leaned towards bringing him along, although in moments of self-searching honesty he recognized it was mainly a selfish impulse so as not to have to face the family alone.

There was even some talk of bringing Stevie along, but this raised several concerns, not the least of which was having a total stranger show up at the Carmody residence to inform the bereaved parents that their beloved son was now a horse residing in Kentucky. Even if that did not sound completely crazy, there was the minor logistical issue of getting Stevie away from her jockeying duties and explaining to her dad and Mr. Jenkins that she needed to visit an unknown family for a secret reason with two young men they had never heard of before. So the Stevie option was nixed.

Although he would never admit it to a living soul, in moments of weakness Mike sometimes thought it would be good if Necromancer lost the races or maybe even had an injury (nothing life-threatening of course) so that he could avoid the task entirely.

Whenever he entertained such thoughts he afterwards beat himself up for his selfishness and cowardice. Besides, he thought the right thing to do no matter what was to let Hal's family know. Any way you slice it, it's still a miracle of sorts, Mike reasoned, and he would want to know regardless of the circumstances. Did it really matter whether Hal was a racing superstar or just a working nag on a farm?

As February approached, everyone was busy. Sid and Eleanor making plans for a May wedding, Stevie and Ed O'Neill getting Necromancer ready for the Fountain of Youth, Hal himself getting back into racing focus, and Seth and Mike making plans for the big visit and what in God's name they were going to tell Hal's family.

CHAPTER TWENTY-SIX

Although Sid's routine at the VA hospital had become pretty regular, he still had at least one new experience every day he showed up. As they say in the war, business was brisk, and for every soldier discharged from the hospital it seemed like there were two ready to take his place. Sid's dad had fought in WWII, and although it sounded like anything but a walk in the park, there seemed to be a clarity of purpose and spirit that was largely missing from the boys he spoke with at the hospital. His dad would talk about Hitler and Mussolini like they were evil comic book villains who needed to be vanquished by the Justice League. But most of these kids didn't seem to have much of a clue what they were fighting for, other than some vague notion of "promoting freedom," or "preserving democracy," whatever that was supposed to mean. Sid himself was no dove, and believed in a strong offense being the best defense. But even he was beginning to have grave doubts about the wisdom of sacrificing so many for a cause that no one seemed to be able to articulate, and with sides that seemed to morph into new sides, friends who turned into enemies and vice-versa. Or maybe it was just the relentless sadness of witnessing the after-effects upon these young men and women.

On this particular day, he was working in the cafeteria, doing a bit of everything-helping with the meal prep, serving to the doctors and soldiers, bussing tables. He noticed a pretty young girl working at the serving station who looked about sixteen or seventeen. Truth was, Sid had found it harder and harder to get a fix on the young women of the present, with kids looking like adults before their time. Eleanor just chided him for being a grumpy old guy, but even she admitted that it was kind of sad how fast kids grew out of being kids these days. And they were in full agreement that the proliferation of the "cell phone zombies" was a plague upon society. Sid got so sick of dodging these people who couldn't bear to tear themselves away from their devices even for a nanosecond to see where they were going, that he sometimes bumped into them on purpose, just to remind them that they still resided on planet Earth.

To her credit, this girl seemed fully engaged with the people around her, smiling and making conversation. Sid was heartened to see that. The girl, Petra, was doing her best to keep up her smile and banter in the face of some difficult sights. She had gotten more used to seeing the injuries and so had hardened herself to them as much as possible. It was sad to say, but the toughest part of volunteering was the condition (imposed by her teacher and supported by the VA) that she could not have her cell phone with her while working at the hospital. She got a fifteen-minute break every couple of hours and frantically raced to her locker to get at the phone and see the critical information she was missing out on, such as who had what for lunch or what irrelevancy had been posted on her friends' Facebook or Twitter page.

While Sid and Petra were engaged in their own thoughts, a youngish soldier entered the cafeteria. He looked to be in his late twenties, tall, well-built, handsome in a rugged sort of way, with short brown hair and matching eyes. As he grabbed a tray and headed down the chow line, Sid could discern no scarring or injury, but there was something about the faraway look in the young soldier's eyes that made Sid think that he might be one of the head cases. Sid had seen quite a few of the patients who were suffering from some sort of PTSD. He had never heard his dad talk about any of his fellow soldiers suffering from that, although he imagined that diagnosis had come a long way since the 1940's. In any event, he knew that although there was no outward physical manifestation, PTSD could be as debilitating as losing a limb, sometimes worse.

As the soldier reached Petra's station, she smiled and asked him what he would like. He nodded at the mashed potatoes and she gave him a heaping spoonful. As he turned to head towards the rows of tables, he stumbled and dropped his tray, with the clanging making those in the cafeteria look up at once. Petra left her station to go and help the soldier pick up the tray and plates. As she leaned down to help him, he suddenly jumped back a step and produced a large hunting knife, and started waving it at her in a menacing way. As Sid was closest to the end of the service station, he ran out and got between the soldier and Petra, and tried to calm the soldier down. "Whoa, hey there buddy. We're all friends here. Let's get you a new plate of food and we can sit down together and have a chat, okay?" The soldier, who Sid later found out was Corporal Lance Griggs, seemed momentarily to calm down. But as Sid moved closer to get Cpl. Griggs to put down the knife, Griggs unexpectedly lunged at Sid and plunged the knife between Sid's chest and shoulder blade. Petra screamed, and three members of the staff grabbed Griggs and subdued him.

For a second, Sid was too stunned to know what happened or to feel any pain, but that passed quickly and he was in such agony that he soon passed out.

Fortunately for Sid he was already at the hospital, so they were able to remove the knife and stop the bleeding before things became life-threatening. It would be months before he could lift his arm over his head without much pain. Once he was out of surgery and resting comfortably in his room, he was groggy but just awake enough to see Eleanor by his bedside, smiling and crying at the same time. "Hey, hero. Aren't you a little long in the tooth to be doing the 'Ahnuld' imitation?" Despite his pain Sid managed a laugh, although when he tried to reach out to touch Eleanor's hand he grimaced and shut his eyes in agony. Eleanor kept up the witty banter to try and keep him distracted from the pain. "You know, I'm sure there were less painful ways to get out of a marriage proposal. All you had to do was ask!"

Eleanor stayed with Sid until he fell back to sleep, and was there as much as she could be over the next couple days. On the third day he had another visitor. "Hi, I'm Petra. I think you saved my life." Sid waved this off with the arm he could manage to lift, and Petra continued "Anyway, I just wanted to thank you so much. You were amazingly brave and I was scared out of my mind. And I'm so sorry you got hurt on my account." Sid, still a bit woozy from the pain meds and with a dry throat, managed to rasp out "My specialty is damsels in distress, so think nothing of it, young lady. Just another dull day at the VA." Petra smiled at this and leaned over to give Sid a kiss on the forehead. "I hope you get out of here soon. Rumor has it the food sucks. Seriously, thank you *so* much again. If there's ever anything I can do for you, just ask."

As Petra was leaving, Eleanor passed her coming from Sid's room. She entered with a mock frown and her hand on her hip and said "So now that you're a big hero you're looking to score with the young hotties and dump the old broad?" Sid rasped a dry laugh and said "Gotta strike while the iron's hot!" He explained about the girl in the cafeteria and Eleanor commented that it was sweet for her to have stopped by. They chatted for a while and watched a bit of TV on the microscopic screen the hospital provided until Sid succumbed to the morphine and drifted off.

The next afternoon while Eleanor was there, Sid had two more visitors, Frank and Melody Carmody. Melody introduced herself and her husband and they both profusely thanked Sid for saving their daughter and for his bravery. Sid was both touched and embarrassed by the attention, and thanked them for the lovely flowers and box of chocolates. After they left, Sid had a nagging feeling that he knew them somehow, but between the pain and the drugs he lost his train of thought and soon drifted back to sleep.

Both Sid and Petra had gained a sort of celebrity as a result of the attack. As with seemingly everything else in the world, the incident had been captured on somebody's cellphone, and the video had gone viral, especially in Lincoln. Everyone wanted to talk with Petra about it, even the boys who otherwise wouldn't have noticed her in a million years. The school principal even mentioned it in an assembly and applauded her bravery. Petra was slightly jazzed but mainly mortified by the announcement. She chuckled to herself that she was basically being glorified for being in the wrong place at the wrong time.

Sid got a feature in the local paper. A kid who looked about twelve came to interview him for the story. He also multitasked as the paper's photographer. Sid did his best to mumble out responses to the kid's questions, and was impressed with the kid's command of hyperbole when Eleanor read him the article the next day, mockingly emphasizing the parts of the article referencing "breathtaking bravery" and "answering the call above and beyond his sense of duty." Sid gave her a hurt expression and said "It's nice to see some accurate news reporting for a change."

When Sid was discharged from the hospital a couple days later, Eleanor insisted he stay with her. "This way, I won't have to worry about you. And given your still-healing wounds and the state of your apartment, I'd be afraid of what kind of horrible infection you might subject yourself to." Sid did not put up much of an argument, looking forward to a little TLC from the future missus.

While he was in the hospital, he had been visited by two police detectives, Ainsworth and Colley. Ainsworth was a middle-aged graying brunette with an overbite and piercing green eyes. Colley was a large black man, bald as a cue ball, but with a gentle way about him and a warm smile. Ainsworth did most of the questioning, and Sid related the incident the best he could remember. When Sid asked what was going to happen to Cpl. Griggs, Ainsworth told him that Griggs had been charged with aggravated assault and attempted murder. When Sid protested that he had no interest in seeing Griggs go to jail, Ainsworth looked surprised and said "A few inches to the left and we'd be doing this interview by way of a séance. You really want to see this guy walk?" Sid responded "Look, the kid was obviously not right in the head. I see it too much around here. The war does some seriously screwed-up things to these guys. So to answer your question, no, I don't want him moving in next door to me. I want to see him get the help he needs. And I don't see him getting that in jail." At this point Colley interjected "We appreciate your compassion, Mr. Mackey. But we have an obligation to protect the public. Cpl. Griggs will get a full psychological work-up and at that point some decisions will be made. We appreciate your time and wish you a speedy recovery."

In the first couple weeks since leaving the hospital, Sid had heard nothing further from the police and although he was curious, he decided to let sleeping dogs lie, at least for the time being. Besides, he was enjoying all the fussing over and home-cooked meals and very gentle and careful snuggles with Eleanor. Still, something was poking him in the brain here and there, something he was trying to remember from his time in the hospital.

CHAPTER TWENTY-SEVEN

The Fountain of Youth stakes race at Gulfstream turned out to be largely a non-event, albeit a pleasant one for Stevie and Hal. The race originally had nine entrants including Necromancer, and two of the other horses running were also previous stakes winners. The others were a middling sort, having won some lower-level races but not in the same league. Three days before the race, one of the main challengers, Git Yo' Money, Honey, had to withdraw due to an abscess on his hoof. The day before the race, the other main danger Hellzapoppin also withdrew due to a hairline fracture of his right front leg. This left Necromancer in with a fairly weak field, and he ran to his even-money odds, winning the race by a comfortable four lengths. In truth, he could have won by at least twice that distance, but coasted down the stretch so as to preserve energy for the other upcoming races which were certain to be more difficult. Ed O'Neill was very pleased to see this, and commended Stevie on her racing smarts, once again giving her credit for something she had nothing to do with.

In addition to the nice financial gain, the win also provided valuable points for the Derby qualification, giving the team some margin for error in the upcoming races. O'Neill thought that might well come in handy, as the Rebel and especially the Blue Grass were likely to be much more competitive.

So while Hal was looking forward to March and the Rebel stakes, Mike was making plans for a far less exciting but undoubtedly more challenging visit to Lincoln. He and Seth had made travel arrangements coinciding with the spring break period, so as not to raise undue suspicion about the visit. They agreed to come in the day before they told their families they were coming and share a hotel room near the airport, so that they could work out the finishing details on their plan to discuss "the Hal situation," as they had begun to call it, with the Carmodys.

While Mike and Seth were planning their clandestine activities, Sid was sitting up in bed, having remembered what was bothering him at the hospital. He got up and turned on Eleanor's computer, put in her security-lame password (her birthday), and went to a search engine to find the article on his attack. He found the original article from the local paper, and scrolled down until he found the name of the young girl at the center of the incident: Petra Carmody. It was not the most unusual name, but it struck a resonance with Sid, and now he thought he knew why. He started another search, this one about a tragic car accident which had taken the life of a young man. It took him a bit longer to find what he was looking for, but finally he came upon an article entitled:

"TRAGIC DEATH OF LOCAL TRACK STAR TEEN"

He read the article and saw that the boy's name had been Hal Carmody, and a shiver went down his spine. He carried on reading, despite his strong desire to leave those memories in his deep subconscious, and came to the fateful section:

"Mr. Carmody is survived by his parents, Francis and Melody, and his sisters, Alison and Petra."

Sid just sat there numbly staring at the computer screen. When he finally snapped out of his trance, he was overwhelmed with thoughts: First, how he had finally gotten some much-deserved punishment for what he had caused (although in his opinion he had still gotten off far too lightly-maybe a few inches to the left would have been fairer?). Second, that to the extent there was some higher force pulling the strings down here, he had an even more insane sense of mischief than even Sid could have imagined.

But the one that needled him that day and for every subsequent day was this: What do I do now that I know about this? The simple (although admittedly spineless) answer was "absolutely nothing." After all, there was no bringing the boy back, was there? And wouldn't coming forward merely serve to poke at healed wounds and cause nothing but harm? So while undoubtedly self-serving, this option could not be dismissed out of hand.

On the other hand, here was a family that had fallen over themselves thanking him for saving their daughter's life (which he still did not believe was the case) and telling him they were in his debt. Would they still feel this way if they knew of his involvement in their son's death? Didn't they have a right to know?

He really wanted to talk about this with Eleanor, but he was desperately afraid that she would tell him to get out of her apartment and never speak to him again. Of course, if he decided to confront the family, he would in all likelihood have to tell her anyway, since it would come out one way or another. And a part of him, the "old" Sid, thought he deserved to lose Eleanor as part of his punishment for the past. He thought of June and what she would have told him. She probably would have said he should come clean, that keeping dark secrets bottled up could only lead to bad things.

Just to get himself back to some equilibrium, he decided to table the issue for that day, and made no mention of it when Eleanor came home. He recognized that this was not a long-term solution since it would bother him like some sort of buzzing mosquito in the night until he did something about it.

The following day, after a largely sleepless night, he came to a decision. He would tell Eleanor, relationship be damned, and do whatever she said he should do: Nothing. Tell the family. Take a long walk on a short pier. When Eleanor got home that evening, Sid had a grim look on his face and asked Eleanor to take a seat. Her first thoughts were either than he was calling off the marriage or that he had been diagnosed with some terminal illness. Sid took hold of her hands and said "There's something I need to tell you. I'm not proud of it. I know you have some inkling of my life before we met, but you need to understand how bad it had gotten. After June died...actually even before June died, my life had spiraled pretty far down the old toilet bowl. I drank way too much. I gambled money I could ill afford to gamble with. And while that was sad, it was okay as long as I was only destroying myself, especially after June passed away. But one day a few years ago, I was drowning my sorrows at a bar downtown, and was pretty stewed by the time I left. I stumbled into the street and was nearly hit by an oncoming car. It would have been better if I had been."

At this point Eleanor was looking at him gravely and squeezed his hands and said "Don't ever talk like that, Sid. You're scaring me." Sid continued. "The reason I say it would have been better if the car hit me is that after it missed me, it hit a boy and killed him." He looked up and saw the shocked expression on Eleanor's face and nodded. "It took me a long time to get over that, if I ever really did. Anyway, I thought I had until recently. So, my little adventure in the cafeteria, right? The girl who I 'saved,' her name is Petra Carmody. She had a brother named Hal, got hit by a car and killed. Same family, and yours truly is there to balance the scales."

Eleanor looked down at her hands for a long minute, and then up at Sid. Instead of being angry or disgusted with him, she came close and put her hands on his shoulders and kissed him. "Sid, you poor, poor man. Beating yourself up over this all this time. You didn't kill anyone, and you certainly did not mean to harm that boy. For all you know he could have got hit whether you were there or not." Sid was not sure he agreed with Eleanor's view of the facts or her logic, but he was relieved she didn't hate him. She went on. "Crazy things happen. People die in all kinds of weird, Rube Goldberg-like ways. Neither one of us is in line for sainthood, and I don't know much about faith, but if there is some master plan than this was part of it. And maybe if you get hit and killed instead of the boy, the daughter gets stabbed to death by a disturbed veteran. Who the hell knows?"

Sid felt a million percent better than he did just an hour ago. He asked Eleanor what she thought he should do about the Carmody family. She didn't hesitate. "Just let it be, Sid. To them you are a hero, and you are to me too. Why blacken that good feeling and dredge up old pain? What is it that you think you will accomplish? Do you need their absolution?" Sid pondered this and finally said, "I guess I feel like a bit of a fraud, taking all their praise for saving their daughter without taking my share of the blame for their son's death. And no, I don't need absolution from anyone but you."

Eleanor ended the conversation by saying "It's of course entirely up to you, Sid. You are the one that has to feel right, that you've done the righteous thing. I'll love you whatever you decide. But if you do decide to confess, just know that you might do nothing more than add to their pain, so make sure you are doing it for them and not yourself."

CHAPTER TWENTY-EIGHT

The important thing about the Rebel stakes at Oaklawn was that it would be an excellent gauge of where Necromancer stood, as at least five possible Derby horses would be joining him at the starting gate. The unfortunate thing was that it was in Arkansas, which meant a long ride to a place no one seemed particularly excited to go. Stevie had asked Mr. O'Neill why he had chosen that race, and O'Neill explained that the journey, the unfamiliar track and the quality of the field would help to toughen up Necromancer in preparation for the Derby.

Unlike the trips to New York, there was no sightseeing on the agenda for this trip, which was probably just as well, thought Stevie. The only things she knew about Arkansas was that it was where former President Clinton was from, and that they had some hot springs.

The race would be run at the same distance as the Fountain of Youth, so everyone was confident that

Necromancer would be fine with the distance. He didn't seem too much the worse for wear from the travel and looked healthy. Ed O'Neill had dinner with Stevie the night before the race, and told her not to push Necromancer too hard. He knew this was the best competition the horse had yet seen, and as long as the horse placed reasonably well they would be fine in terms of qualifying points. When Stevie asked for some clarification, O'Neill said "I'm not saying don't try to win the race. I'm just saying that if it does not look like that is going to happen, don't overexert the horse down the stretch just to gain a placing. The most important things are that he comes out of the race healthy and with some more experience under his belt."

Stevie related O'Neill's comments to Hal, who was not overly happy. "I thought the whole point of this is to win the race? He makes it sound like I'm some china doll you have to pick up carefully or it'll break." Stevie told him to calm down and said "I don't think that's what he means at all. What I really think is that he believes you are the best chance he might ever have to win the Kentucky

Derby, and he just doesn't want anything to happen that would hurt your chances. We are going to go out there to try and win the race, end of story." Hal was mollified by that and they moved on to other subjects. "I've been talking to your friend Mike and I think he plans on seeing your family this month. So keep your hooves crossed they don't treat him like an insane patient. If all goes well, hopefully we can arrange a reunion sometime soon." Once again Hal thought about what a great friend Mike was to undertake this, and although the whole prospect was unnerving, he was excited by the thought he might see his family sometime soon.

There were thirteen horses entered for the Rebel stakes, and although Hal was not overly superstitious, he was a bit relieved when one of the horses had to withdraw, making it a field of twelve. Necromancer had drawn the far outside post, and so both he and Stevie were intent on getting into a better position from the start. As the gate opened, Necromancer went out fast and managed to get into fourth position, about three-wide from the rail. As the field hit the halfway point, he remained fourth, about three lengths from the leader and a length and a half from the second and third place horses. Two other horses had settled about a half length behind him.

As they made the final turn for home, the lead horse had tired and was being passed by the field. Necromancer had moved into second place behind one of the favorites, Cavalry Dan. Closing quickly behind him was another favorite, Cheezhead, who Hal and Stevie were told was owned by a former star quarterback for the Green Bay Packers. As they entered the final hundred yards, there was little separating the three horses, and Hal found a bit in reserve as they approached the finish line to win by a half-length, with Cheezhead second and Cavalry Dan third.

By winning the two races Necromancer had already qualified for the Derby, and at the rate he was going he might even be the favorite. So barring a disaster, things were looking hopeful for the Holyrood team.

CHAPTER TWENTY-NINE

In the days following the race, the Carmodys received two sets of visitors, each with unsettling tales to tell.

The first of these visitors was Sid and Eleanor. They were surprised to hear from Sid, but happy to invite him to their home after what he had done for Petra. After Sid decided he needed to do this, Eleanor volunteered to accompany him and Sid was grateful for the company. Sid put on his best suit, which he had worn exactly twice in the last ten years, and immediately felt ridiculously overdressed as Frank Carmody answered the door in a Chicago Bears sweatshirt and jeans. He shook hands vigorously with Sid and more gently with Eleanor. Frank led them to the kitchen where Melody was making coffee and laying out some cookies. She gave both of them a hug and welcomed them to her home.

After some small talk and inquiring about how Petra was doing , Sid began to explain why he had come. He started by saying "Sometimes in life we get credit for things we don't deserve it for, and sometimes we avoid blame for things we should be blamed for." He saw the puzzled looks from the Carmodys and continued. "I don't believe Corporal Griggs would have hurt your daughter. I'm glad we never had to find out. And after talking to Eleanor I'm not sure if I'm to blame for this other thing, but I didn't feel right not telling you about it."

Sid went on and retold the tale of what had happened on the day that Hal had been hit by the Porters' car and killed. The room was so quiet both during and after the telling of the story that Sid truly believed you could have heard the proverbial pin drop. After an uncomfortably long silence, Melody composed herself and spoke. "Mr. Mackey, first let me say that I admire your courage for coming here to tell us about this. I can only imagine how difficult that was for you. As far as Frank and I are concerned, you saved our daughter's life and we will always be grateful for that. As for our son, I'm sorry that you have been blaming yourself for that all this time. There is no sense to make out of what happened that day. A thousand things could have gone just a tiny bit different and he would still be with us. And believe me, I've been over each and every one of those until I thought I would lose my mind. And although I did not know until today of your part in all of this, it doesn't change anything. We will always love and miss Hal. Thankfully, and in no small part due to you, we still have two beautiful daughters to raise."

At this point the emotions in the room were palpable, and Sid's head was bowed. He finally looked up and said "I can only hope to possess a tiny bit of the grace you have in your heart, Mrs. Carmody. Your words mean so much to me, and I am so grateful for your understanding." Frank Carmody, who had said nothing during the entire exchange, finally spoke up. "Sid, I teach science, so I don't know much about faith or karma or any of that stuff. I deal in proof. But whether you look at this scientifically or spiritually, if you had gotten killed by that car instead of our son, you wouldn't have been there that day to protect Petra."

After thanking the Carmodys again for their understanding, Sid and Eleanor took their leave. On the drive back to Eleanor's place, she said "You know, I thought it was the wrong thing to come and risk confrontation or reopening old wounds. But I was wrong. What wonderful people they are. And here I am, with my wonderful man." She leaned over to give him a kiss on the cheek, and saw that Sid had tears welling in his eyes.

At the same time Sid and Eleanor were meeting with the Carmodys, Mike and Seth were checking into an America's Best Inns and Suites near the airport. Upon entering the lobby, Mike felt that the name of the hotel was a gross overstatement. When they got to their room, he decided that it was a criminally or at least civilly actionable falsehood. The room had a funk to it somewhere between a peep show and a cigar bar, and Mike resolved to sleep fully clothed. Seth commented that although they were unlikely to find a minibar in the room, they might find several species of household pests. Still, for $39.95, he guessed you could not expect the Ritz.

They decided to go down to the restaurant in the hotel, which was only slightly less depressing than their room. They ordered cokes and burgers from a waitress who seemed as excited as they were to be there, and began discussing plans for the following day. Mike began by saying "Seth, don't take this the wrong way, but I think it's best if I do most of the talking. I need you there to back up my story, and frankly, because I'm scared out of my wits to be doing this. But as you can gather, it's a pretty delicate situation, and 'delicate' is not your strong suit." Seth pulled a face but to his credit did not rise to the bait.

"My plan is just to tell the story as straightforwardly as such a story can be told. Either they'll believe it or, more likely, they won't and never speak to either of us ever again. But it's all we can really do. My hope is that the story is so incredible that they have no choice but to believe us. After all, who would be crazy or sick enough to make up something like that?" At which point Seth grinned and raised his hand.

They had contacted the Carmodys on the pretext that they were coming home for spring break and wanted to stop by to say hello. While she was happy to hear from them, Melody did find it a bit curious that they would call ahead and schedule a time to meet with her and Frank. She wrote it off to the boys' being sensitive to the situation with Hal.

On the ride over the next evening, Mike and Seth had serious somersaults going on in their respective stomachs. All the planning they had done seemed a folly now that they were actually approaching the Carmody house. They got out and rang the doorbell, and still found it strange that Hal himself would not be coming to the door. Instead, it was Frank Carmody who greeted them both with handshakes and manly half-hugs. Melody emerged from the kitchen and gave them both more motherly hugs.

Mike was grateful for the time spent catching up on respective family matters, with he and Seth talking about their college experiences. Seth, to his credit, did not whine about Syracuse, instead focusing on his work with the communications department and his first experience standing before strangers and telling jokes at an open mic night. Although he had been telling jokes since he could first talk, Seth admitted being terrified standing up in front of strangers. He said it was fortunate that most of the patrons were pretty drunk, as the laughs came a little easier that way. Melody commended him on his bravery, relating a story about her first appearance in court and how she threw up before going into the courtroom.

Mike, for his part, told them that he loved Duke. It was a great school with a lot of sprit, especially the so-called "Cameron Crazies" who made every basketball game a wild experience. He was thinking about going into law, as he realized early on that being a star athlete at a small high school was not a precursor to being drafted in the NFL. He had made the football team as a reserve, but by his sophomore year it was clear he was never going to start, so he decided to focus on his studies. Mrs. Carmody told him that law was not for everyone, but that the training would serve him well no matter what he ultimately decided to do.

The conversation shifted to the girls, and Frank said they were doing great, with Petra looking at colleges, and joked that he would have to take a night job at 7-11 to keep them out of the poor house with tuitions as high as they were. Mike had been told by his mom about the incident with Petra, and gingerly asked about it. Melody admitted it had been very frightening, but that a nice man had luckily been there to intervene. This brought back memories of her meeting with Sid Mackey, and she couldn't resist. "Mike, Seth, you remember the day of the accident?" They both nodded and looked down and she continued. "Do you remember seeing an older man crossing the street in front of the red car?" Mike responded "Honestly, Mrs. Carmody, I don't remember seeing anything until that car was right on top of us. I only looked up because the tires were squealing." Seth confirmed that he too had seen nothing until the last second, omitting that he had been ogling a young woman in a short skirt on the other side of the street.

Grateful for the opening about Hal and not having to make it himself, Mike dived in. "About Hal..." Suddenly everything he was going to say floated out of his head. He regrouped. "What do you think happens to us when we die?" he asked. Both Frank and Melody looked at him curiously, and finally Melody said "Well, both Frank and I were raised in the church, and so we were taught what everyone else is about heaven and hell. But I'm a lawyer and Frank's a professor, so I think it's fair to say we share a healthy skepticism about the teachings of the church. So to answer your question Mike, I honestly don't know. For Hal's sake I hope all that stuff about heaven is true. What do you think?"

Mike looked intently into Mrs. Carmody's eyes and said "What if I was to tell you I knew what happened, at least in one particular case. Would you believe me?" At this point Mr. Carmody tried to lighten the mood and said, "Whoa, Mike, this is all starting to sound a little spooky, did you..." but he was cut off by his wife, who was staring at Mike as intently as he had stared at her. "Sure Mike, I'll believe you. So tell me what you know."

Mike swallowed and realized how dry his throat was and asked Mrs. Carmody for a glass of water. After taking a long drink, he looked up and prefaced his story by saying "I know how unbelievable this is going to sound, but I swear on my family's life that it's true." Mike then went on to tell the story, from the first letter he had received from Stevie to the visit to the farm and everything else that had taken place. When he finally finished and had the courage to look at Mr. and Mrs. Carmody, he saw vastly contrasting expressions. Mr. Carmody looked ready to smash Mike's face in, and Mrs. Carmody had a look encompassing awe, sadness, hope and wonder.

As Frank began to thunder about "what a lousy thing to do," Melody grabbed his hand and told him to stop, which he reluctantly did. She turned to Mike and said "Mike, I've known you since you were a baby. You have always been mature beyond your years, and you were always a great friend to Hal. But as you can imagine, this is a hard thing to get my head around. I know you would never play a cruel joke on us like this, but is it possible that this girl, for whatever reason, is playing one on you?"

At this point Seth, who had not said a word during the whole exchange, and who could not even bring himself to look up during it, finally said. "I don't think so, Mrs. Carmody. When we went to visit the horse Stevie claimed was Hal, we asked questions only Hal would have known the answer to, and he answered them all." Melody asked Seth "So he actually talked to you?" Seth grimaced and said "Well... not exactly. He communicates telepathically with Stevie, and she provides the answers." At that, Frank got up and said "Okay, I've heard enough. I can't begin to imagine why anyone would do this but I'm not listening to another word of this nonsense." Melody tried to hold him and settle him down but he was having none of it, and went off to his study and slammed the door.

Melody sat back down and apologized on behalf of her husband, but Mike waved her off and said that he probably would have reacted the same way. The three of them sat in silence for a time, and finally Melody said "I don't know whether to be thrilled that Hal might still be with us or horrified that someone would pull such a cruel trick on us. I can't imagine why a girl from Kentucky who assumedly has no reason to do so would engage in such a deception. But as a lawyer, I'm trained to gather and evaluate facts and draw conclusions from them." She then got a legal pad and pen and asked Mike and Seth for all the information they had, which was not a lot. She then wrote on the pad:

NECROMANCER?

STEVIE RAINES?

HOLLYROOD FARMS?

And below that.

HAL?

CHAPTER THIRTY

While Hal and Stevie were preparing for the last of the Derby prep races, the Blue Grass, Melody Carmody was putting on her lawyer's hat and doing her own investigation into Mike's story. After the boys had left, Frank came out of his study and offered a sheepish apology to his wife. "I don't know what came over me. I guess there's a spot in my soul that is still raw, and I just reacted from the gut to Mike's story. It was stupid. I know as well as you do that Mike would never intentionally do anything to hurt us. I still don't believe his story, but I believe that *he* believes it." Melody gave her husband a kiss and said "I don't know what to believe. But just dismissing the story without more is hardly an option at this point. So I'm calling in sick tomorrow and doing my own digging into this."

And that she did, first buying an online subscription to a publication called the Daily Racing Form, which seemed to have the most comprehensive information on horses. Once she was signed up and logged in, she was easily able to find Necromancer. She was first directed to his prior race history, which was a chart with all sorts of mysterious and confusing entries, and she managed to find a glossary which helped explain what all the abbreviations and numbers meant. She was no expert, but she did see that the horse had done pretty well in its races, at least more recently. She also saw a symbol that suggested that the horse was eligible for the upcoming Kentucky Derby, and was duly impressed.

Of far greater importance, she found the lineage information on the horse. She had to stop and take a deep breath when she saw that the birthdate of the horse was the same day that Hal died. She also found the name and location of the owner of the horse, Holyrood Farm in Lexington, Kentucky. There was no specific address, so Melody opened another tab and Googled Holyrood Farm. She found a website for the farm and when she opened it, there were various tabs for "breeding," "sales," and "careers." She located a "contact us" link and clicked on it, and found a phone number and address which she wrote down. She looked for information on Stevie Raines but could not find anything.

She navigated back to the Racing Form site and was able to find a few bits of information on Stevie Raines. She was a jockey for Holyrood and had been riding Necromancer since his third race. But that was pretty much it. So far, everything that Mike told her had checked out. She chewed on her pen and thought about next steps in her investigation.

As a lawyer, she knew that the element of surprise was often important in getting to the truth. Well prepared witnesses generally had their stories down pat, true or false, like actors in a play. It was the curveball that often tripped them up, the question neither they nor their lawyer saw coming. She knew that it was much harder to lie on your feet than by following a script, so she wanted to make sure that when she confronted this Stevie Raines the girl did not have time to prepare. She thought about just flying down and visiting the farm unannounced, but saw at least two potential problems. First, she couldn't be sure she could gain admittance without some sort of appointment. Second, even if she could, there was no guarantee that either Stevie or Necromancer would be there on that particular day.

She finally decided on the best approach and called Mike. She explained what she needed Mike to do. After listening to Mrs. Carmody, Mike hesitated and finally said, "Okay, I'll do it. Stevie will probably be pretty mad at me for springing this on her, but I know how important this is for both you and Mr. Carmody...and Hal. I'll arrange to visit the farm and meet with Stevie and Necromancer, and I won't mention anything about you coming." Melody thanked Mike and hung up.

After making the arrangements with Mike, Melody's next task was to come up with a list of questions she could be confident there was no possible way this girl could know the answers to. She was aware that in the internet age, there was a wealth of information available to anyone with the time and expertise and (sometimes) money. She was also aware that, however unlikely it might be, this girl could have a relationship with someone in Lincoln who might have known Hal growing up. So whatever she was going to ask about had to be things that only she and Hal would have been privy to. While this seemed straightforward at first, she actually struggled to think of the type of intimate questions that were required to either confirm or debunk the girl's story. As she was trying to come up with those questions, she stopped at one point and laughed a bit crazily, thinking how insane this whole endeavor was.

The next day Mike tried to call Stevie but was unable to get ahold of her. He left several messages over the next few days and was starting to fear that she was no longer talking to him for some reason. Finally, he got a call back from her, and she apologized for not returning his call sooner. "It's been crazy around here with all of the preparation for the Blue Grass and hopefully the Derby," Stevie said "Between the workouts and grooming and meetings with Mr. O'Neill our trainer, I rarely have a moment's peace. So, anyway, what's up Mike?" Mike explained that he wanted to visit Hal again sometime soon, and was put in a quandary when Stevie said "I'm sorry, Mike, it's really not a good time now. The Blue Grass is less than two weeks from now, and as I said it's a bit crazy around here. By the way, have you spoken to Hal's family yet?" Mike swallowed and composed himself before baldly lying to Stevie. "No, not yet, still waiting for the right moment. That was one of the reasons I wanted to come and see Hal again." Stevie was silent and Mike wondered if she had cottoned on to his fabrication. Finally she said, "Okay, I'll find a way to get you in next week before we leave for Keeneland. I'll let you know tomorrow what day you can come." Mike thanked her and said he would wait to hear back. As promised, Stevie called the next day and told Mike he could come the following Thursday, before she and Hal travelled to Keeneland on Friday.

Mike immediately called Mrs. Carmody and told her about the planned visit. After hanging up with Mike, she jumped back on the internet and was appalled to see how expensive the flights were on short notice, but shrugged her shoulders and pulled the trigger, figuring there was no price to be put upon a reunion with your talking horse of a son. After making the flight arrangements and finding a nearby hotel, she called Frank and told him about the plan. He was less than thrilled for several reasons, since it would mean cancelling a late semester set of classes and having to come up with an excuse for doing so, all for what he viewed as a fool's errand. Still, he understood how important it was for Melody (and in truth, himself, if for no other reason than to achieve closure) and so he mumbled something about conjuring up a dead relative's funeral to tell the dean. After he hung up, he realized how deeply he had just thrust his foot into his mouth.

The last major task was telling Petra and Alison about the trip. They decided there was no point in letting the girls know anything about the discussion with Mike and Seth, at least until they had determined whether there could possibly be any truth to it. So they came up with a story about a college roommate of Frank's who had passed away suddenly and that Frank felt obligated to attend the funeral. Petra in particular was skeptical of this story, asking her dad why he had never mentioned him before, and when was the last time he had seen him. Before Frank could get too tongue-tied (he was a terrible liar in Melody's experience, which she took comfort in from a marital standpoint), Melody changed the subject and told them about the visit they had from Sid Mackey, omitting the details about his confession. As Petra was old enough to watch Alison, there was no need to get a sitter. Both Petra and Alison whined about the arrangement, but eased off a bit when Melody told them they could order in Chinese or pizza or whatever they wanted the nights she and Frank would be away.

Unbeknownst to Frank and Melody, being of the generation that used the internet without fully investing themselves in it, Petra, who remained suspicious about this purported last minute funeral of some guy she never heard of, went on the computer when her parents were asleep and went through the browser history. She knew her mom had no idea about deleting her search history or any of that stuff. She was totally mystified by what she found: A subscription to something called the Daily Racing Form and research on some horse farm in Kentucky. She had never known her parents to be either gamblers or horse people, so she was at a loss to understand why they were looking this stuff up. She found it curious, though, that the horse farm was coincidentally in the same city where this alleged funeral was to take place.

The following Wednesday, Frank and Melody agreed to meet Mike at the airport. For obvious reasons, they did not want the girls to see Mike joining them for the trip. They had purchased a ticket for Mike, adding to the exorbitant price of the short trip. After they had left for the airport, Petra went to her parents' closet and saw that the three suits her father owned were sitting on their hangers. Bullshit confirmed, she thought.

CHAPTER THIRTY-ONE

When the three of them arrived at Holyrood Farm, Mike turned to Mr. and Mrs. Carmody and said "Please let me do the talking. I will explain to Stevie why we did it this way and hopefully get her to understand." The Carmodys agreed to let Mike handle the situation. When Stevie arrived at the main house, she was taken aback to see that Mike was not alone. Given the two older adults with him, and being no fool herself, Stevie surmised that these were Hal's parents. Stevie gave Mike a dirty look, and before things got unpleasant, he pulled Stevie aside.

"Look, I apologize for springing this on you and not telling you the truth. As I'm sure you can imagine, it was not an easy conversation to have with Hal's folks. And Mrs. Carmody insisted that we not announce their visit ahead of time." Stevie glared at Mike and said "I can't believe you would lie to me like that, telling me you hadn't even spoken to them! Don't you trust me?" Mike fumbled for words and finally said "Yes, of course I do. But I'm not sure about the Carmodys." Stevie shook her head and replied "Then why should I try to help them if they don't even trust that I'm telling them the truth? Don't they realize how far I've put my own neck on the line here?" Mike nodded and said "You have every right to be angry. But just put yourself in their shoes for a minute. They're told that their son, who they presume has been dead for three years, is alive and well as a horse in Lexington, Kentucky. If the roles were reversed, wouldn't you be the tiniest bit skeptical?"

Stevie chewed on this for a bit and said, "Okay, I guess I can see that, although why I would lie about such a thing is beyond me. And the only reason I can think of for them popping this surprise is to try and catch me off guard, which presumes I'm lying about the whole thing. And that seriously pisses me off. The only reason I won't send them on their way is Hal. He deserves to see his family. So skip the introductions and just follow me."

Mike went back to the Carmodys and whispered for them just to follow along and not say anything. Melody thought it was rude that Stevie would not even say hello to them, but kept her counsel as she could sense the girl was none too happy with the situation. Good, she thought, I want her a little angry. That's when most people tend to make mistakes. During the long walk to the stables, the Carmodys took in the sights and sounds and smells of the farm, the horses walking about, the grass and horse droppings, and the occasional whinnying. They had to admit it was a lovely setting.

When they finally reached the stables, Stevie put up a hand signaling for them to wait outside, along with a glare that said she was not messing about. She went in and found Hal snacking on a carrot she had left for him earlier that morning. "Hey, buddy. I'm sorry to spring this on you so suddenly, but you have visitors." Hal noticed her use of the plural and assumed it was Mike and Seth. "Well, you have that half right, anyway," Stevie continued. "Mike is here. Uh, along with your mom and dad." Hal's head snapped up so quickly that Stevie was afraid he might have injured himself. He said "I *can't believe* you didn't tell me before that they were coming!" Stevie held her hands out in protest and responded, "Whoa, I'm just the messenger! I found this out all of fifteen minutes ago myself. Apparently your mom has a preference for ambush. Anyway, it's entirely up to you. I'll shed no tears sending them on their way if that's what you want." Hal responded that was hardly an option and just asked for a minute to compose himself.

When Stevie led Mike and the Carmodys back to Necromancer's stall, the first thing Hal noticed was how much his parents had aged in three years. His dad was thinner and more fragile looking, and well on his way to baldness. His mom's hair had gotten noticeably greyer, either that or she had stopped bothering to color it. There were also more prominent wrinkles around her eyes and mouth. He didn't doubt that he was in large part to blame for the rapid aging. After getting over the shock of seeing them, he went over and nuzzled each of them, the best he could do since hugging would have to be a one way option.

Melody Carmody finally spoke to Stevie. "I'm sorry that we had to do it this way. Please don't be angry with Mike. He was just trying to be helpful to me. I'm the one who asked him to lie to you. I'm not proud of it, but it was the only way to satisfy myself whether this unbelievable story could possibly be true. I sense you are angry with us, but I hope you will do the right thing and help us find the truth." Stevie pursed her lips but nodded. Melody told her that she had a few questions to ask...she couldn't bring herself to use her son's name, not yet. "Fire away," Stevie said.

"First, when my son was a baby, he had a blanket that he carried with him everywhere. What did he call it?" Hal heard the question and thought to himself, "Great, the one question I have no idea of the answer to. Leave it to mom to ask me something from eighteen or nineteen years ago when I was like two!" He wracked his brain but could not for the life of him come up with it. He told Stevie and she related to Melody that he did not remember. She pulled her skeptical lawyer's face and proclaimed "How convenient!" Stevie was tempted to tell her where she could put her convenience, but managed just barely to hold on to her temper.

Melody then asked "When my son was about five, there was a big accident in our house. What caused it?" This one Hal remembered vividly. They had a poodle named Simon and the two of them were constantly running around the house after each other. It was around Christmas, and Hal had Simon on a leash and was going to take him for a walk along their yard. But Simon darted away and managed to get his leash tangled up in the Christmas tree. When Hal went to yank the leash, the tree came crashing down, and hit him in the face, opening up a nasty cut that ultimately required five stiches. It also sent Christmas balls and tinsel flying everywhere. After momentarily being furious with him, his mom saw the cut and ran over to hug him and grabbed some kitchen towel to stem the bleeding. She grabbed Hal and they recklessly drove to see Dr. Hanson who stitched Hal up while he screamed loud enough to wake the dead.

Hal related the story to Stevie, who repeated it pretty much verbatim to Melody. She put her hand over her mouth while her eyes simultaneously bugged out and filled with tears. She thought to herself there was no way this girl could have known about the story, unless she was a secret friend of Petra's, which seemed highly unlikely. Meanwhile, Frank Carmody looked as if he had seen a ghost, which he later reasoned that he had. After taking a long time to compose herself, Melody finally asked the question that she was a thousand percent sure that no one in the world but Hal could know the answer to.

"My son and I used to play a little game with each other. I would whisper in his ear a question and he would whisper back to me his answer. Mine was 'If cats eat mice and mice eat cheese, what does cheese eat?'" Without any hesitation, Stevie said "Cheez Doodles." Melody Carmody screamed "OH MY GOD!" and rushed over to hug Hal's head. Frank stood stock still for a moment, still processing the insane notion that this four-legged beast in front of him was his son. Finally he joined the hug-fest and everyone in the stable was crying, including Mike and Stevie.

Melody couldn't stop saying "Oh my god" over and over again. When she had finally managed to recover a modicum of equilibrium, she started asking Hal a bunch of rapid-fire questions about how he was, what he remembered, was he being cared for. Finally Stevie had to stop her and say "One at a time, please. It's hard enough to hear him over all this racket, better yet trying to answer three questions at once." Melody apologized and forced herself to slow down. Hal, through Stevie, responded that he was well and enjoying his life as a racehorse, although he obviously missed being human and being with his family. He asked about Becca, and Melody told him that she had gone on to UCLA, and seemed to be doing well. They had heard from her quite a bit in the year after the accident, but not so much now, although she managed to stop by at Christmas.

After many questions and answers were exchanged on both sides, Stevie apologized and told the Carmodys she needed to take Hal out for a final training run and then to get everything ready for the trip to Keeneland. She explained about the race and about the Kentucky Derby, and Frank was extremely proud to hear that his son would be participating in the Derby. Melody asked about Keeneland, and Stevie explained that it was very close by. Melody turned to her husband and said "Frank, we have to stay and go to the race!" Frank mused about the headaches of arranging yet more coverage with the dean and telling extended lies to their daughters, but knew it would be impossible to deny his wife's request. After giving Hal a final hug and promising to see him again very soon, Stevie led Mike and the Carmodys back to the main house. Before they left to go back to their hotel, Melody pulled Stevie aside and said "I don't know how to begin to thank you for what you have done, or to apologize for the way I treated you. You have given a mother the greatest gift she could ever receive-a chance to be reunited with her son. There is no way I could ever repay that debt. All I can say is THANK YOU *SO* MUCH." She hugged Stevie and kissed her on the top of her head. Stevie was crimson and momentarily at a loss for words. She finally managed to say "We all love Hal here and I know how much this means to him. Things are going to be hectic here for the next couple of months, but after that we will figure out how you can all be together as much as possible."

On the ride back to the hotel, Melody alternated between thanking Mike and peppering him with more questions about Hal. He was relieved when they finally reached the hotel so he could chill out by himself for a while. He begged off dinner that night, feigning a stomach ache, not sure he could endure another session of thanks and questions.

CHAPTER THIRTY-TWO

Everyone was on pins and needles heading into the Blue Grass. Ed O'Neill just wanted to see a solid performance from Necromancer heading into the Derby. And please, *please*—no injury. Stevie's head was still a bit cluttered by the recent events with Hal's mom and dad, and she was trying to refocus on the race. And of course for Hal's parents, they were about to see their son race again, albeit in a completely different context. It had been many years since either of them had been to the races, and they were both enjoying the revelry and bustling nature of the crowd. They bought two programs from a grizzled old vendor at the entrance to the track, one to look at and pretend to handicap the races, and the other to keep pristine for the day they told Petra and Alison about what they had learned.

The only one who wasn't nervous was Hal. He had every reason to be. The race, his parents watching, the final prep for the Derby. But he was operating on all cylinders, still flying after the reunion with his mom and dad. He was barely thinking about the race, until Mr. O'Neill made his usual trip to the stall about an hour beforehand. There was not too much discussion about the race, as they had been aware for several weeks about the quality of the field, and likely how the race would set up. O'Neill's main message to Stevie was to take the race as it came, not try to do too much. He would of course be happy if Necromancer won, but he was more concerned that the horse come out of the race in good fettle.

When the horses came out for the Blue Grass, Melody and Frank got up to clap and cheer for their son. They moved down to the rail so they could be as close as possible when the race finished. Hal looked around and saw his parents, and his adrenaline was pumping as the horses approached the starting gate. When the gate opened Stevie almost fell off Necromancer as he burst out flying. Necromancer opened up a three length lead almost immediately, which was both impressive and worrying, given that two of the entrants were confirmed front-runners. The lead had extended to five lengths by the half-mile mark, and although the horse had previously won wire to wire, O'Neill understood that the prior race had come against lesser competition.

Hal was feeling great as he breezed around the track, seemingly by himself. He was already thinking about the prideful looks on his parents' faces as he crossed the finish line. Unfortunately, he was still more than a quarter mile from the finish, and suddenly he could feel the thundering hooves of his competitors getting closer. As they headed into the final turn, Necromancer's lead was down to a length and dwindling. Hal reached for that extra pocket of reserve... and his body came up empty. After the fifth horse had passed him Stevie gave a gentle pull on the reins, a signal to just get to the finish line safely. Necromancer finished eighth out of the ten horses that started the race.

The excitement the Carmodys experienced as their son was romping over the field soon dissipated as the other horses passed him. Although Frank was clueless as to what had occurred, Melody still possessed a mother's intuition, and she thought that perhaps Hal had felt too much pressure and tried too hard knowing they were there. She felt bad about it, and resolved to talk to Stevie about whether it would be better if they didn't come to the Derby.

Ed O'Neill was more incredulous than angry when he found Stevie back in the stalls. "Can you explain to me why you would run our horse so ridiculously fast over six furlongs in a race that still had four furlongs to go?" Stevie knew better than to answer. O'Neill continued "I don't mind so much that we lost the race. I told you that beforehand. What I do mind is you risking our Derby chances by running the horse at a suicidal pace. I know you know better than that." Before Stevie could respond O'Neill just shook his head and walked off. Stevie turned to Hal and said "Thanks, buddy, for making me look like the world's biggest idiot. What got into you?" Hal sheepishly lowered his head and replied "If it's any consolation, you could only be the world's second biggest idiot. I was just so psyched to have my parents watching me race again that I completely lost the plot. When I got out to that huge lead I was feeling so great, and then the bottom just sort of dropped out. Anyway, I'm sorry. I love seeing you get the credit when we win but it's totally unfair for you to get the blame when I screw up so royally." Stevie patted Hal on the nose and said "That's okay. I guess I got so used to you controlling things that I forgot that technically, at least, I'm supposed to pay attention to the actual race. So there's plenty of blame to go around."

It was a short but uncomfortable ride back to Holyrood, with Ed O'Neill saying very little. He was angry about the race, but even more than that he was bracing himself for yet another discussion with Leroy Jenkins about who should jockey the horse for the Derby. Fortunately it was late enough when they returned that the discussion would be put off for at least one more day.

Sure enough, the following morning Jenkins found Ed O'Neill at the training track and asked Ed to join him for lunch that day. O'Neill already knew he wouldn't have much of an appetite. As he entered the dining room with its large oak table and impressive chandelier, he saw that just the two of them would be dining. Plates of fried chicken, biscuits and corn on the cob were laid out, and Ed took one of each, knowing it was more than he would finish. Jenkins, after chewing and swallowing a large bite of chicken, turned to O'Neill and said "Ed, no sense rehashing the race. We both saw what we saw. You convinced me once to stay with Stevie and I'll admit it's worked out pretty well. But I think we both saw that she's still green at this game. And I owe it to everyone here to give us the best chance to win the Derby next month. So I already spoke to Frankie's agent yesterday and although he has a mount for the Derby, he's willing to get out of that obligation to ride Necromancer."

O'Neill started to object, but Jenkins put his hand up and said "We've been through this argument before, Ed, and I have no interest in doing it again. It's not very often that I pull rank around here, you know that. But I've got to put my foot down on this one. Since it's my decision I'm happy to take it upon myself to tell Stevie. I know it's going to come as a big disappointment to her." Ed waved him off and said "No, it'll be better coming from me. I still think you are making a mistake, but after the Blue Grass I'm not even sure myself anymore." With that he got up, leaving his meal untouched.

CHAPTER THIRTY-THREE

As April was winding down, plans were being made and then remade. For Sid and Eleanor, the marriage in Kentucky was proving logistically more difficult than originally imagined. For one thing, finding any sort of decent hotel rooms for friends and family was nigh on impossible, and the few rooms they could find would cost almost as much as the wedding itself. Ditto for trying to find a restaurant to accommodate fifty-plus people on the Sunday night. Eleanor kicked herself for being so naïve about how busy Lexington would be, and there were serious thoughts about cancelling their plans and instead doing something in Lincoln later in the month.

Frank and Melody had been struggling with how to go about telling their daughters about their brother. The discussion had started as soon as they had left Holyrood, with the preeminent question being whether to tell them at all. While this seemed like a non-issue to Melody, Frank disagreed. "We need to think about what this will do to the girls, Melody. Petra is just getting over the trauma of almost being killed, and Alison is still a child in many ways. They have managed to cope with their brother's death, and now three years later we're going to tell them 'Oh, he's not really dead, he's just a horse now.' Assuming they believe us, we can't know how they will react. Will they be thrilled Hal is still with us, even in his altered state, or will they be horrified that he must live in a barn and can never communicate or do any of the things he loved to do?"

Melody was having none of it. "Frank, I think you are *seriously* underestimating your children. Sure, they will be pretty freaked out at first hearing about this, but who wouldn't? The beauty of youth is its resiliency, and our kids will handle it just fine. And could you imagine how angry and resentful they would be if we didn't tell them and they found out some other way? It hardly bears thinking about. No, there is zero question in my mind that the girls have to be told, and the sooner the better."

After so many years of marriage, Frank knew when there was no point in extending an argument, and clearly this was one of those times. So now that the decision had been made, the next issue was how to go about dropping this particular bombshell. They both agreed to sleep on the matter Sunday after their return, particularly after being set upon by Petra's series of sarcastic questions about the funeral ("So dad, were they upset that you showed up for a funeral in a t-shirt?") which made them aware that at least one of their daughters did not buy their last-minute trip story.

The first thing that set off Petra's radar Monday night was the pizza boxes waiting on the table when she got home from her volunteer work. Her mom was pretty hardcore about home-cooked meals and not eating too much junk, especially knowing that she and Alison had gorged themselves on pizza and Chinese food over the past several days. The second was the quiet, with dinner usually mouthfuls of food between interrogations and spirited discussions about the issues of the moment. The third was the weird kind of glued-on smiles her parents both had on their faces, as if this was some sort of Twilight Zone episode where her parents had been replicated by aliens.

"Okay, what's up?" she asked as soon as she sat down. Melody managed to evenly say "Who says anything's up, young lady?" Petra grimaced and replied "I know you think that beauties like me don't have two brain cells to rub together, but I've been living in this house for seventeen years and I pretty much know when something funky is going on. No offense dad, but if you're going to lie to sneak away for a few days, take some lessons from a teenager next time so you don't seem quite as pathetic trying to pull it off."

Frank put on an expression of mock umbrage and everyone laughed at that, relaxing the room a bit. Melody used that opening to launch into the long story about their brother, finishing with their visit to Holyrood and the questions she asked of Hal through Stevie. For once, Petra was momentarily speechless. It was Alison who had lots of questions ("so he's not really dead?" "When is he coming home?" "How does he like being a horse?") they tried to answer as best they could. When Petra finally regained her voice, she said "If I didn't know you as the most boring parents in the world, I might think you were on some pretty serious drug binge. But since I also know you as the loving and supportive parents you are, I know you wouldn't tell us this unless you were one-hundred percent sure it was true. So, I guess the only question is when are we going back to see him?"

Melody hesitated as both of her daughters looked expectantly at her. Finally she explained about what had happened at the Blue Grass and how she felt that Hal might have lost the race because of them. "It's only a couple weeks until the biggest race of his life and I'm wondering if we should just let him be for the time being and wait for a while before we go see him." "No way!" Petra exclaimed. "You can't tell us about this and then expect us to wait for a month or two to see him. If you were going to do that, you shouldn't have told us at all!" Frank gave Melody an 'I told you so' look which Melody returned with an exasperated one. She turned back to her girls and said "Here's the deal. I'm going to talk with Stevie and see what she thinks. She's closest to Hal now, and she will know better than anyone whether his chances will be hurt if we come back to see him before the Derby. So whatever she says goes. You can be as mad at me as you want, but I'm not going to ruin Hal's chance to win the biggest race of his life." The tone of her voice said she would brook no argument, so Petra and Alison glumly ate their pizza in silence.

When Melody tried to reach Stevie the next day, she had no idea that Stevie was in the midst of a discussion that would change the course of hers and Hal's future. She knew something was up when Mr. O'Neill and Frankie showed up in Necromancer's stall early that morning. O'Neill in particular had a grim expression on his face, and was holding his hat so tightly between his hands you would have thought it was going to bite him. Frankie smiled and said hello but she could tell he was equally uncomfortable. She tried to break the tension by saying "So, to what do I owe the pleasure of being visited by two handsome gentlemen this morning?" But O'Neill continued to look grim as he said to Stevie "There's no easy way to say this so I'm just going to come right out with it. Mr. Jenkins has decided that Frankie will ride Necromancer in the Derby. It's not fair and I don't agree with it, but it is what it is." Stevie was stunned. Frankie tried to soften the blow. "Look, Stevie, there isn't a jock out there who doesn't think you've done a fantastic job riding this horse, most of all me. When you've been around as long as I have, you'll understand this is a cold business. Mr. Jenkins is a good man, but even he is not above covering his own behind. If he loses with me aboard, no one will raise questions. So it's not about you or your riding skills. It's about everyone covering their behinds."

Stevie told Frankie he had nothing to apologize for. "I don't blame you for anything, Frankie. You have a chance to ride a Derby winner and you'd be a fool to turn it down. And by the way, gentlemen, while I appreciate your decorum, I believe the appropriate term is 'covering your asses.' And Mr. O'Neill, you've been a great friend to me since this whole thing started. I know you did your best for me. And you can tell Mr. Jenkins I'm not angry with him. If it wasn't for him I wouldn't be here anyway. I'm disappointed, to put it mildly. But the most important thing is for Necromancer to win, so just let me know what you need."

O'Neill, although not a man of wide range of emotions, was greatly touched and impressed by Stevie's reaction, and before leaving said to her, "No offense to Frankie, but I'd pick you to ride my horse anytime, kiddo. Leroy's making a mistake. And I'll let him know that again for all the good it will do. You take care now."

After Frankie and O'Neill left the stall, Hal said to Stevie "I'm not racing." Stevie turned to Hal and said "Don't be stupid. Of course you are. It's the freaking Kentucky Derby, for christsakes!" Hal, in a voice as serious as a wake, said "I...Don't...Care. If you are not riding me I'm not racing. They can force me into a trailer and lead me to a stall and put me in the starting gate, but that's as far as it'll go." Stevie looked horrified and screamed at Hal "YOU CAN'T EVEN THINK ABOUT DOING THAT! Do you have any idea what an embarrassment that would be to everyone here, me included? Now stop being such a baby. After all, I'm the one whose getting screwed here, not you." As soon as it left her mouth she knew it had been the wrong thing to say. Hal confirmed that when he rejoined, "Exactly. After all you have done for them and especially for me, they dump you at the last minute for something that wasn't even your fault. I'm sorry if I *embarrass* them but that's exactly what they deserve. You can talk until you're blue in the face but my mind is made up. Either you ride me or I don't run."

Stevie was touched by Hal's loyalty but terrified that he might actually go through with his plan. She gave him a couple hours to cool off, but when she visited him later that afternoon, he was even more obstinate, and she was at a loss as to how to proceed. When she finally had a moment to check her phone, she saw that Mrs. Carmody had left several messages. Although not in much of a mood to speak with her, Stevie thought that maybe Hal's mom might have a suggestion on how to get through his thick skull. She returned the call and Mrs. Carmody answered on the first ring.

"Hi Stevie, thanks for getting back to me. I have an important question for you. My daughters now know about Hal and want to visit before the race. But I don't want to do anything to hurt Hal's chances of winning the Derby, so I wanted to have your thoughts on how you think it might affect him. I also wanted to ask you if it would be too much of a distraction for him if we were all to come to the Derby."

Stevie couldn't help but to laugh to herself and then said, "Mrs. Carmody, at this point I'm not sure any of that matters." She then went on to explain what had taken place that morning and Hal's reaction. After a lengthy silence, Melody replied "Oh, dear. That's not good. I'm sorry for you both. Hal always was a bit stubborn when he felt something was wrong. I wouldn't put it past him to stick to his guns. On the other hand, he's always been super-competitive, so maybe he'll change his mind and go out there to win?"

Stevie pondered that and said, "Well, I'm not too keen on leaving it to chance. At this point, I can't see the harm in having you all come down. Maybe you can convince him to stop his foolishness and come to his senses. How soon could you make it here?" Melody asked how soon she needed them there, and when Stevie responded "Yesterday," she laughed and said, "Okay, let me see if the gang is up for a road trip. My husband will be thrilled at taking more time off of work and the girls will be over the moon about a fourteen hour car ride, but it sounds like we don't have a whole lot of choice. Unless you hear from me, expect us there tomorrow by around four o'clock."

After hanging up with Stevie, Melody immediately called Frank at his office. After listening to his wife, Frank said, "I'm sorry, hon, I just can't do it. It's finals week and I am already treading water after missing three days last week. I don't want you driving in the middle of the night with the girls. Can you get flights out there?" Melody replied,

"Not happening. Nothing available today. Besides, who would dare tangle with a lawyer and two teenage girls?" Frank was not amused, and reiterated what a bad idea it was. But Melody was undeterred, and said that they would be fine. After cutting off the discussion with Frank, she called Petra who surprisingly was totally on board with a car trip. "Cool, mom. Can we stay in one of those hotels with the mirrored ceilings and vibrating beds?" Melody responded, "No, but we can eat crappy highway food and stay at the Norman Bates lodge." Hearing no response from Petra, she realized her daughter was a bit young for the Psycho era.

Although she was less keen about taking Alison on a long and unfamiliar drive, she knew it was pointless to try and keep her at home. The yelling and tantrums and post-tantrum resentment were too much to think about. So the ladies (who Melody jokingly referred to as "Thelma and Louise and Alison"-totally lost on the girls) got in the Carmody mini-van, plugged in the address of the farm on the Garmin, and headed out for their adventure, armed with an over-supply of diet cokes and chips and Cinnamon Toast Crunch for Alison.

They reached the halfway point in the journey by around one a.m., and found a relatively non-scary looking Red Roof Inn off a highway exit, where they were able to get a room. Although everyone was exhausted by then, the intake of too much diet coke left the three of them unable to fall asleep, so they put on the TV. The HBO channel was showing the movie Secretariat, with Diane Lane, and they all agreed that was a hopeful omen. Melody fell asleep before the girls, and was rewarded the next morning by mocking imitations of her snoring.

After grabbing breakfast at a McDonald's next to the motel, they got back on the road. As they crossed over into Kentucky, there was a palpable feeling of excitement from the girls, and Melody refocused on how strange this was going to be for them, hoping they would manage. She called Frank to let him know all was okay and that they were nearly there. According to the Garmin, they were less than an hour away. Melody called Stevie to let her know they were en route.

As she turned into the now familiar road leading to Holyrood, Melody saw Stevie in the distance waiting at the main house. After they parked and got out, Stevie immediately motioned for them to follow her, without any introductions or niceties. As Melody and the girls ran to catch up with her, Melody grabbed Stevie's arm and asked her what was wrong. Stevie replied, "Things have gotten a little weird around here. I don't know if it's the Derby or whatever, but everyone's keeping a close watch on Necromancer and I'm not sure they would welcome a visit from strangers, so it's best if we just hustle along and get this over with."

When they reached the stalls, Stevie checked to see that they were alone and then motioned for Melody and the girls to join her. She apologized for having to rush them along, and introduced herself to Alison and Petra. Melody in turn introduced the girls to Stevie. Petra thought that Stevie was cute in a tomboy sort of way. Alison asked Stevie where her brother was, and Stevie smiled and led the way to Hal's stall. When Petra and Alison entered the stall, Hal immediately leapt up and nuzzled the girls, and Alison laughed like a child as she put her nose against his. Although Petra was normally concerned with maintaining her cool exterior, she couldn't stop the tears from coming. She asked Hal how he was, and, through Stevie, he told her he was great, especially now that they were there. Alison had tons of questions about being a horse, all of which Hal answered patiently, throwing in some humor about the size of his poops and missing his Nikes. At one point Petra glanced downward and stifled a surprised laugh, telling Hal he would be hugely popular with the ladies. Melody grimaced and apologized to Stevie, who only laughed and said not to worry, the "hung like a horse" jokes were pretty common around the farm.

After all the questions were answered, Melody told Hal why they had come, and pleaded with him to come around. "Look, I know you're stubborn, and I take full responsibility for that trait. And I agree that what they are doing to Stevie is totally unfair. But you must know that doing what you are planning will hurt so many people, including us. We want you to succeed in whatever you do. And of all the things you aren't, 'quitter' is right at the top of the list."

Hal listened to his mother and eventually responded. "This isn't about quitting or trying to hurt anyone. It's about standing up for what I think is right. You and dad always taught me that was one of the most important things anyone could do." Melody replied, "Yes, Hal, we did teach you that and nothing you do in this life or any other makes us more proud. But it's not just about standing up for what is right, it's *how* you go about doing that." As Hal remained adamant about his position, it was Petra who suddenly figured it all out. She beckoned for her mother and Stevie to follow her out of the stall and outside while Alison fed Hal some carrots. "Guys, it's not Hal being so stubborn about doing the right thing. Don't you see it? He *loves* her," pointing to Stevie. "He's just pissed off that she is being treated like this, and so he has dug his heels...uh...hoofs in the ground. So mom, you can use all your lawyerly arguments on him, but I don't think it's going to make a bit of difference. Funny as it sounds, I think this is about a man standing by his woman."

The three of them pondered that, and Stevie had to admit that she and Hal had shared a special relationship since he was born, although she had never seen it in exactly those terms. Melody was impressed with her daughter's intuition and told her so. Petra waved that off and said "Mom, you've been with dad so long you probably never think about infatuation the way girls my age do. And remember, Hal's basically still a teenager at heart."

Understanding Hal's underlying motivation did not necessarily create a roadmap to a solution. If anything, it made it harder, as emotion-based decisions were much more difficult to overcome. They rejoined Alison and Hal in the stall, surprised to see Alison atop her brother. Alison was beaming as she held tightly to his neck. Stevie laughed and said "Looks like you are ready to ride your brother in the Derby!" As they were distracted by the goings on, they failed to hear Mr. Jenkins and Mr. O'Neill enter the stalls to check on Necromancer. As they entered his stall, Jenkins exclaimed, "Who in the hell are all these people?"

Stevie introduced Mrs. Carmody and her daughters. Jenkins gave a perfunctory hello and then turned back to Stevie. "Stevie, you should know better than to bring strangers around here without clearing it first, especially now. What could you have been thinking? Ed, please escort these folks out. I need to speak with Stevie alone." As O'Neill motioned for the Carmodys to follow him out, suddenly Stevie yelled at the top of her lungs, "STOP!" Everyone turned around at the violence in her voice and involuntarily obeyed. Stevie continued. "Pull up a couple of stools, Mr. Jenkins. I have a story to tell you and it's going to take a while."

CHAPTER THIRTY-FOUR

Three things stopped Leroy Jenkins from refusing Stevie's request. First, he had a genuine fondness for the girl, going back as far as the first time they met. She always struck him as a bit of an underdog, and he saw a lot of himself in her, struggling from a lowly groom hand himself to owning one of the more successful horse farm operations in the country. Second, she seemed so angry and intent, which was very unlike her normal gentle spirit, so he thought whatever she had to tell him might be important. Third, he was just darn curious.

So Jenkins and O'Neill found a couple stools around the barn and sat their behinds down on the uncomfortable things. Jenkins hoped it was a short story as his butt began to ache pretty much the second he sat down. Unfortunately, it was not a short story, but by the time Stevie got rolling Jenkins had forgotten completely about his sore bottom.

Stevie started from the beginning, when Hal first spoke to her and she thought she was going crazy. From there she talked about her research, how Hal had died at the same time that Necromancer was born. How Hal told her things only he could have known about his friends, the accident, his family and other stuff. How his friends Mike and Seth came to visit and asked him questions only he could have known the answers to. How Hal had continued to talk to her through the races. Why he stopped when Frankie used the whip on him. Why he tried too hard in the last race, because his mom and dad were there. And finally why he was refusing to race in the Derby.

Before either Jenkins or O'Neill got a chance to speak, assuming they could have mustered the ability to do so, Melody interjected. "Mr. Jenkins, Mr. O'Neill, I'm a lawyer. While that hardly makes me immune from being a fool, I can assure you I am not. I could get you a hundred testimonials from clients and colleagues and judges to confirm that. Now, I'm also a bereaved mother, or at least I thought I was, so I'll be the first to admit that I'm not exactly a neutral observer here. But I will tell you something, and you can believe it or not. I came here a week ago to find out whether this young lady was either the cruelest little trickster God ever created, or whether she was telling the truth. I asked that horse over there questions only my son could have known the answers to. I am so convinced that this horse is my son that I brought the two most precious possessions in my world down here to see him. So as incredible as this story sounds, I am telling you with not a shred of doubt in my mind that your horse Necromancer is also my son Hal."

Jenkins and O'Neill sat there silently, seemingly waiting for the other to speak first. Finally, Leroy Jenkins looked at Stevie and said "Well, if you wanted to ride the horse that badly in the Derby, you could have just asked me to change my mind! I like to think I'm an open-minded fellow, but this is pretty crazy stuff, you got to admit." Ed O'Neill interrupted him at that point and interjected, "You know, Leroy, it might explain a couple of things. Like why the horse stopped the two times Frankie rode him. And more than that, I've seen this horse make so many smart decisions on the track, putting aside the Blue Grass debacle. I thought it was just natural instinct, but who knows."

Jenkins was undeterred. "Now, my wife is the big churchgoer, but I know enough about what's supposed to happen to us when we die. We either go to the good place or the bad place. What we don't do is get put into horses or dogs or pigs! What it sounds like to me is a whole lot of coincidences that somehow got twisted into this crazy story you all have bought into. Now, Mrs. Carmody, you seem like a nice lady. And I'm very sorry for your loss. But believing this nonsense isn't doing the memory of your son any good. And Stevie, you've always been a good kid and a real asset around here, so I'm just going to try and forget about this whole thing." With that he slapped his thighs and told O'Neill it was time to go.

Suddenly, Necromancer leapt up and started whinnying loudly, blocking their exit before bolting out of the barn. They all chased after him as he went into the practice track. He was moving back and forth and side to side with a strange motion and by the time they caught up with him, Jenkins and O'Neill stopped dead in their tracks as they looked into the practice track and saw that the horse had crudely spelled out in the dirt:

STEVIE RIDES OR I DON'T

CHAPTER THIRTY-FIVE

Leroy Jenkins, who truth be told needed to lay off the parade of fried foods he so adored, had to be helped back by Ed O'Neill to the main house, as he was faint and his heart was racing at dangerous RPMs. Martha Jenkins greeted them at the door and asked what was wrong, and O'Neill muttered something about it being a long story and asking her to bring a cool towel and some water. When she returned, she saw three more strangers along with Stevie Raines, and said in an excited voice, "Would someone please tell me what in tarnation is going on?" Melody introduced herself and her daughters and apologized for intruding upon their home. Martha momentarily regained her composure and Southern charm to welcome them, and then began badgering Ed O'Neill again about what was going on.

After getting a cold towel on Leroy's forehead and getting him to take a few sips of water, O'Neill finally turned to Martha with a pained expression and said, "Martha, you wouldn't believe me if I told you. I think Leroy's going to be fine, but probably best if you call a doctor just to be on the safe side." Martha ran off to find Dr. Turnblatt's number, knowing he would come straightaway as he and Leroy had known each other going on forty years. While she was making the call, O'Neill turned to the four of them and said "That's the goddamnest thing I've ever seen." He seemed ready to say more but just shook his head and went back to Jenkins' side.

As she anticipated, Dr. Turnblatt was by Leroy's bedside within twenty minutes of her call to him. After examining Jenkins, he came downstairs and told Martha that her husband would be fine, but that they should let him rest for a few hours. "And maybe get that man to eat a vegetable now and then," he added tartly before writing out a prescription and telling Martha to call if there were any further episodes.

Martha invited the group into the library and had some iced tea brought in for her guests. After everyone was comfortable, she turned to Ed O'Neill and again asked what had happened.

O'Neill squinted and instead of answering pointed a finger in the direction of Stevie. Everyone turned in her direction, and Stevie haltingly began to speak, for the second time that day telling the incredible tale of how Hal came to be resident at Holyrood. Of course, she had a brand new ending to the story in light of recent events.

When she had finished, Martha Jenkins had a bemused look on her face, as if she was the butt of a practical joke. She turned expectantly to Ed O'Neill, expecting him to restore a bit of sanity to the conversation, but all O'Neill had to say was, "Martha, I can't attest one way or the other to the rest of the story, but you are welcome to walk out to the training track and see it for yourself." Martha Jenkins opened and closed her mouth a couple of times, and ultimately just pursed her lips, folded her hands in her lap and closed her eyes with head bowed. When she finally raised her head, she turned to Stevie and said "You know, it's funny. I remember you coming to the library that time and asking for my help looking up information on that boy. At the time, I thought it was just some teenage girl thing. I've been a lifelong Christian and never much doubted the church's teachings, but I've got to admit I'm not sure even Father Caldwell could explain this one away."

When Melody told Mrs. Jenkins that she and the girls would leave them to head back, Martha would hear nothing of it. "It's late and you have a long journey ahead of you. I insist you stay the night with us. We have plenty of room and you'll feel fresher in the morning. I'll have Mary fix us up a light meal and go see how my Leroy is doing." When she returned, she told them that he was sleeping and that she did not want to disturb him. Stevie got up to say her goodbyes. Hugs with the Carmodys were exchanged and she thanked them for coming on such short notice. Melody laughed and said "Well I guess it's a good thing we did! We'll all have quite a story to tell, not that I'm sure anyone will believe us!"

After sitting down for a simple salad and some grilled chicken with rice and beans, Martha showed them to their rooms, which were somewhere between quaint and opulent, with rustic furniture co-existing with expensive-looking vases and chandeliers. After the excitement of the day and with food in their bellies, the three of them had no trouble falling asleep. They were roused by the activity in the household the next morning, and Petra was horrified when she looked at her watch to see that it was only 5:30 am. She found her mom and Alison blearily rubbing sleep from their eyes, and they wandered downstairs in their pajamas, greeted by the glorious smells of eggs frying in butter and bacon on the grill. Leroy Jenkins was already sitting at the table reading the newspaper. When Melody asked him how he was feeling, he put the paper down and said, "Physically, I feel fine. Not so sure about my mental faculties, though." From the kitchen Martha called out, "Leroy, I'm sure you are as sane as the day I met you, whatever that means. Now stop your complaining and offer your guests a seat." He did as told and they all sat as Martha Jenkins and Mary brought in plates of bacon and eggs and toast.

As they sat down to eat, Mr. Jenkins asked Melody about Hal and what had happened to him. She didn't dwell on the accident, instead focusing on what a great son he had been, and his exploits in track. When she had finished, Jenkins said "He sounds like a wonderful young man. And if he's now with us, hard as that is still for me to believe, then we will do everything we can to make sure he is well cared for."

After cleaning up and getting ready to go, the three of them thanked the Jenkins' for their hospitality and started to leave. Before they reached the front door, Leroy Jenkins pulled them aside and said "I want you to join me in my box for the Derby. My assistant will arrange for your hotel and transportation, and she will meet you at Churchill Downs the morning of the race. I think it's important that you be there." Melody was overwhelmed by the generosity of his offer and thanked him for it. "Nonsense," he said, "It's you I should be thanking."

That afternoon, Jenkins met with Ed O'Neill. "Well, Ed, I guess you get your way after all. Who am I to argue with a horse that apparently can understand English and write with his hooves?" O'Neill issued a dry chuckle and said, "Leroy, us two old goats have seen just about everything, but I doubt either one of us in his wildest fantasies could have conjured up what happened yesterday. And I'll tell you, as crazy as all this seems, I feel like we've got a real shot at taking this thing, knowing what we know now." Jenkins gave a non-committal shrug and replied, "I guess it could go either way. A stubborn horse is one thing. One with human emotions is something else entirely. Anyway, we'll know in a week or so. I'll call Frankie and let him know. If he can't find another mount on short notice, I'll find some way to compensate him."

When he called Frankie later that day, he was somewhat taken aback by Frankie's response. Frankie laughed hysterically and finally caught his breath and said, "No problem, Mr. Jenkins. I didn't want you to think that I had lost my marbles, but Stevie had already shown me her special horse's 'talents.' So I'm probably one of the few people who wouldn't call the state mental health department on you. And to tell you the truth, I'm relieved. Of course I'm disappointed to miss out on the ride, but Stevie deserves to ride that horse, and now I'm more certain than ever that she'll give you the best chance of winning the race. So good luck to you all."

After thanking Frankie for his understanding, Jenkins undertook his final task for the day. He found Stevie grooming Necromancer and called her aside, as he was still a bit spooked by what the horse had done yesterday. He knelt down so they were eye to eye, grabbed her shoulders, and said "Good luck in the Derby, kiddo. We're all counting on you. And tell that stubborn bastard over there that after being such a pain in the ass, he better goddamn win that race!" She gave him a big hug and felt like she was floating on air as she told Hal the news. Hal just nodded and nuzzled her and told her not to worry, there was no way they were losing that race.

CHAPTER THIRTY-SIX

Back to her somewhat normal life, Melody was doing the weekly food shopping at Safeway when she literally bumped into Eleanor Dobbs, crashing carts as she turned a corner towards the cereal aisle. After apologizing without looking up, she sneaked a glance and saw it was Eleanor. "Fancy running into you here" she said with a smile. Eleanor laughed and said, "Yes, it is. Glad we didn't meet on the road." Eleanor grimaced as she realized what an incredibly stupid and insensitive thing that was to say, but Melody charitably glossed right over it and asked how the wedding plans were coming along. "Well, the good news is we found a church to hold the service at. The bad news is we have no place to hold a reception. Leave it to brainiac here to plan a wedding in Lexington on Derby weekend and not bother to book a reception hall like ten years in advance!" Melody laughed and said she hoped they figured out a way to work things out. She then asked if Eleanor and Sid were going to the Derby and

Eleanor said, "Of course we are. That was my big Christmas present to Sid. The horse that Sid says saved his life is running in the race and I knew Sid would want to be there." Melody was intrigued and asked about the horse.

"His name is Necromancer." As soon as Eleanor uttered the name Melody had to grab onto the shopping cart to keep her balance. Eleanor continued ,"I know Sid told you a bit about his life when he came to your house. I wasn't with him at the time but the way he tells it, his life had pretty much hit rock-bottom." Sid had never expressly told Eleanor of his plans to kill himself, but she was smart enough to read between the lines of his story and had figured something like that might have been in his thoughts. "Anyway, he goes to the track one day with all the money he has in the world, which amounts to a few hundred dollars. The name of the horse reminded him of his wife for some reason, so he bet everything he had on it. The horse apparently went off at very long odds and when it won that day, Sid went from penniless to winning over a hundred and sixty thousand dollars. He stopped whatever he might have been planning and slowly began to drag himself up from self-despair. He pretty much stopped drinking and started volunteering at the VA. Then he met me and the rest is history!"

Melody looked a bit ashen and Eleanor suggested they check out and sit down for a cup of coffee at the inevitable Starbucks attached to the supermarket. Melody nodded and after they sat down Eleanor went up to order for them, bringing back two coffees and a blueberry muffin to pick at. Melody thanked her and started to speak and then stopped. Finally she started again and asked Eleanor whether she believed in God. "Well, I'm glad we're keeping the conversation light! Okay, I can see you have something important on your mind. The answer is yes and no. Yes, I would like to believe there is a higher force. It's comforting. But like everyone else I see the senseless cruelty and suffering all around and ask myself the same tired question everyone asks: if there were a god how would he let all this...stuff happen. And since every religion claims it has the one true god, then everyone else must be wrong, huh? So there's my half-assed answer. What about you?"

Melody replied, "I was raised Catholic but my folks weren't overly religious, and Frank and I have followed suit. We go to mass on the big ones but are not heavy duty followers. Look, I know it's a strange way to start a discussion, but I have a story to tell you and so I wanted to know before I started. I need for you to hear this because these series of events are either some sort of divine intervention or coincidences so incredible that any movie studio would reject the script as too unbelievable."

So Melody proceeded to tell Eleanor everything that had happened, from the discussion with Mike to the initial visit to Holyrood to the climax at the second visit. When she finished, she saw such a look of wonder on Eleanor's face. Eleanor smiled broadly and said, "First of all, I believe you. No mother would tell that story unless she unreservedly believed it. And although my recollection of the church's teachings doesn't include reincarnation, there is that little story about resurrection...But I gotta tell you it restores my faith in a higher being. Your son tragically dies and my future husband thinks he caused it. Then your son unknowingly saves Sid's life by winning a race. Then my Sid, who might not be around but for your son, maybe saves your daughter. It's all just too incredible to believe it's just coincidence. So let me ask you, is it okay if I tell Sid?"

Melody paused to consider this and finally said, "Yes, I think he should know. Maybe it will help him. Anyway I leave it up to you. Before you go, let me have your number. I just had a crazy thought and if it somehow works out I need to be able to reach you." So they exchanged numbers and Melody promised to get back in touch.

When she got home, she made a call to Holyrood and managed to get ahold of Leroy Jenkins. She gave him an abbreviated version of the events involving Sid and Eleanor and then timidly made a request. She was delighted when Jenkins said he would be happy to oblige. She immediately called Eleanor and told her the good news, and Eleanor squealed with delight and thanked Melody so many times that Melody finally had to find an excuse to hang up.

While Melody and Eleanor were exchanging their mind-boggling tales, Ed O'Neill and Stevie were putting Necromancer through his final training runs as Derby day approached. The horse seemed to have a newfound reserve of energy and looked fantastic in training. O'Neill had been through enough good horses in big races to know that nothing was guaranteed—a stumble out of the gate, a bump from another horse, or simply a better horse on the day could all spoil your plans. Last minute rain, a lousy post position, you name it. So the best you could do was get the horse as fit and ready as possible and hope it was enough.

As far as instructing Stevie, there was not a lot to say. With nineteen other horses, most of which were top caliber, there was no grand strategy certain to work. And in a field that large, there was certain to be a mix of front-running speed and closers. The most you could do was identify the best of the mix and try to figure out the likely pace scenario. In this case, O'Neill thought there were four main dangers: Luck O' The Irish, Rowdy Street, Little Hero and Shark Bite. Of those four, Shark Bite was the only certain front-runner, but he thought that Little Hero would likely try to set the pace or rate just behind Bite. The other two were likely closers, and both had eaten up their respective fields in their final prep races. So the choice was where to position Necromancer in the field. And really that came down to how quickly the front-runners went off. If the opening splits were too fast, he would be better off in mid-pack or towards the rear. But if the splits were slowish, then he would need to be much closer to the pace. He would have to trust Stevie and the horse to make that judgment.

On the Friday before the race, they packed everyone up and had quite a caravan from the farm to Churchill Downs. Everyone involved was equal parts nervous and excited, except Hal and Stevie, who were focused and in their own zone, as they had been since the day she had reclaimed the mount.

Shortly after the team left Holyrood, the Carmodys' flight to Kentucky took off. Other than Melody, who on occasion had an extravagant client, none of the others had ever experienced first-class travel, with hot towels and hot nuts and all the free drinks they could manage. For the girls it was exciting, having big plush seats and hot fudge sundaes served by the flight attendant. For Frank and Melody, it was just a joy not having some obnoxious kid kicking the back of their seat or being squeezed in between two morbidly obese passengers.

When their plane landed, a man in a suit was waiting in the baggage claim area holding a card with their name on it, and led them to a limousine. They arrived at the hotel and were floored when the bellman led them up to a suite that was nearly as big as their house. There was an envelope on the dresser addressed to the Carmody Family, and inside were fancy-looking badges for admittance to the box reserved for the owners, along with instructions for meeting their driver the next morning. All Melody could manage to say was, "If only life was like this!"

Sid and Eleanor had a slightly less glamorous trip, in cattle class sitting next to a non-stop talking know-it-all who proceeded to talk across the aisle to his companion about the race and how there was no way Luck O' The Irish was not going to win. They then endured an endless taxi line and finally got to their modest hotel room, disheveled and exhausted.

CHAPTER THIRTY-SEVEN

Although Stevie and Hal had been to some famous racecourses and ridden in some prestigious races, none of those experiences prepared them for Churchill Downs on Derby day. There were probably north of a hundred thousand people there, and every one of them seemed to be hooked up to an amplifier. Even in the stalls the noise was pretty overwhelming. So they did their best to distract each other talking about anything other than the race.

For Sid, this was a far cry from a Wednesday afternoon at Lincoln Raceway, scattered about the thirty to forty derelicts with their t-shirts and stogies and crumpled racing sheets, muttering about some asshole jockey or horse that had just screwed them. Non-winning betting slips all over the floor, accompanied by empty beer cans and the occasional pint of cheap whiskey. By comparison, many of the people here were dressed in smart coats and ties, the ladies wearing fancy hats, well-behaved families taking in the grandeur. Instead of cheap beer in plastic cups, there were mint juleps in souvenir glasses; instead of hot dogs that looked like they had been on the rotisserie since the Korean War, there were fancy sandwiches and salads and cakes. For the first time in memory he was wearing a dress shirt and shoes to a racetrack, and Eleanor looked lovely in a flower-print dress. She was wearing the lucky horse pendant. Sid was so taken by the spectacle that he barely bothered to look at the racing form and instead just let Eleanor pick favorite horse names. Of course several of those horses wound up winning, while the handicappers who spent hours studying the forms cursed their bad fortune.

After being ferried to the racetrack and fighting the traffic both to the track and at the entrance gate, the Carmodys were led up to the owner's box. As they were escorted various people looked and pointed at them as if they were somehow famous. It was admittedly a bit of a charge for all concerned. When they got to the box, Leroy and Martha Jenkins were already there and greeted them all warmly. Melody introduced Frank, who felt a little like the odd man out after all the rest of them had experienced. Ed O'Neill tipped his hat and gave them a little wave. Melody pulled Mr. Jenkins aside and whispered in his ear, and he just nodded his head and patted her on the shoulder. She sat down next to Martha and they engaged in a low but animated conversation.

There was a bar in the box along with a buffet, which had standard race fare (hot dogs, burgers, corn, chips), along with some fancier foods (grilled salmon, filet of beef, a bucket of iced shrimp). Alison and Petra were not shy about gorging themselves. As the day went on more people joined them in the booth and introductions were made all around.

Finally it was time for the race, as the band played My Old Kentucky Home and the horses entered the track to warm up. Necromancer had drawn the four post, which was fine with Ed O'Neill, as it put him in a position to save ground while not being penned in against the rail. As luck would have it, his biggest rival, Luck O' The Irish, was in the fifth post position, so the two jockeys and horses would know where the other was. The Carmodys had already purchased their win tickets on number four, along with another set they would keep no matter what the outcome of the race was. When she saw that Ed O'Neill was staying in the box, Melody asked him why he wasn't down on the track. Ed replied, "I went down an hour ago and horse and rider were fine. Other than attaching a motor to his behind, there's not a lot I can do at this point." It took Melody a few seconds to understand he was joking, and let out a belated and nervous laugh. "I've been at this game long enough to know there's nothing to do but sit back and try to enjoy the race. If I've done my job the horse will do just fine. If not, Leroy over there will be sure to let me know. I know this must be nerve-wracking for you and your family. But remember it's just a race." Easy for you to say, she thought to herself.

The noise was so loud as the horses headed towards the starting gate that Hal could barely hear what Stevie was trying to tell him. She finally leaned over and yelled into his ear, "Whatever happens, I'm so proud of you. And I'm sure your family is too. Having said that, let's go out there and kick some horse butt!" Hal nodded and refocused on the starting gate. After a couple of the horses acted up on their way into the starting gate, everyone was finally in line, and as the bell sounded and the gate opened, the race for Hal and Stevie was nearly over before it started, as the three horse swerved out the gate towards them, causing Hal to stumble and nearly go down. He managed to regain his footing, but by that time he was dead last. As anticipated, Shark Bite pounced on the lead, with Little Hero at his shoulder. A couple others also joined the fray, leaving those four about two lengths ahead of the field, and about eight lengths ahead of Necromancer. Ed O'Neill put down his binoculars and bowed his head, cursing his bad luck. He knew this was exactly the type of thing likely to kill any chance the horse had of winning.

Stevie and Hal regained their composure, and although Hal knew it was a bad break, he also knew he had overcome bad breaks in the past. He accelerated enough to stay in touch with the field but not too much to burn himself out too quickly. At the midpoint of the race he sat in ninth, about seven lengths from the leaders, which continued to be Shark Bite and Little Hero. Rowdy Street sat third, followed by Luck O' The Irish. At around the three-quarter mile point, Rowdy Street started to make his move, and overtook Little Hero, still about a length from Shark Bite. Luck O' The Irish was holding steady in fourth.

Necromancer continued to accelerate around horses and had managed to move up to fifth, still about four lengths from the leaders. When he saw Luck O' The Irish make his move, he followed suit, figuring it was time to go for broke. The two of them motored towards the leaders, and very quickly were by both Little Hero and Rowdy Street. But Shark Bite continued to press forward, and Hal was concerned that if the horse did not tire he might have too big a lead to overcome. As they entered the final turn, Shark Bite maintained about a length lead ahead of his pursuers, and Luck O' The Irish and Necromancer were a mere head apart. Halfway down the homestretch there was finally a perceptible weakening in Shark Bite's pace, and Necromancer and Luck O' The Irish were closing fast. With a hundred yards to go the three horses looked to be exactly side by side heading towards the finish, and the crowd was jumping up and down, screaming for their favorite.

Shark Bite had valiantly led from the start, but had little left as the horses approached the finish. Luck O' The Irish was the first to put a head in front, and Necromancer followed. As they neared the last few strides of the race, it was just two bobbing heads seeming to change place with every bob, and as they crossed the finish there was a huge roar followed by near silence as the crowd tried to figure out who had won. The photo finish sign was immediately illuminated on the Churchill Downs tote board.

Up in the box, the Carmody family was collectively hoarse from screaming. In fact, everyone in the box was completely spent, sweating and wringing their hands. Ed O' Neill kept running his hands through the little hair he had left. Melody kept telling everyone how proud she was of Hal whatever the result, getting a few curious glances from those in the box who were not privy to the origin story.

After what seemed like an eternity, the results were flashed: 4, 5, 13, 7. Pandemonium throughout the track. The picture on the TV screens showed that Necromancer had gotten the final head bob and had won by literally a nostril. The box erupted in cheers and hugs and screams and tears as everyone found someone to hug and jump up and down with.

On the track, neither Stevie nor Hal had any idea whether they had won. It had all happened too quickly. All they knew, like everyone else, was that it was dead close. And they knew they had done their absolute best under less than ideal circumstances. But still, they desperately hoped...

When they saw the number four placed first Stevie shot up off the saddle and raised her fists in the air. Before she could compose herself some TV reporter on a horse shoved a microphone in her face and asked her what it felt like to be the first female jockey to win a Kentucky Derby. To the endearment of many millions of people, she replied "Uh, I didn't win anything. I think you are talking about the horse." The reporter laughed and badgered her with a few more questions about the start and how she recovered, and Stevie simply responded that she had the best horse in the world and he could overcome anything.

After the ceremony in the winner's circle and more interviews and still *more* interviews, The Carmody family, Ed O'Neill and Leroy Jenkins met with Stevie in the stall. O'Neill was crying fiercely as he hugged Stevie and told her how proud he was of her. Jenkins got in next to give her a gentler hug and to apologize for ever doubting her. More hugs from each of the Carmodys. It was Ed O'Neill who first turned to Necromancer and said "Well, son, you must think you are pretty hot stuff right about now. Just remember we've got two more little races to win." Hal winked at him and nodded. Leroy Jenkins gave the horse a hug and said "You know, your mom asked me for a favor a few days ago and I was happy to do it no matter what. But after all you have done for us I couldn't be more pleased to grant her wish." Hal was completely mystified by this but was happy that Mr. Jenkins had done whatever it was that his mom asked him to. Jenkins then said, "I'm going to clear out with Ed and Stevie and give you some time alone with your family. And rumor has it that Mrs. Jenkins might be baking an apple pie for our most honored resident tonight." With that, the three of them left, leaving Hal with his family.

Melody hugged Hal and told him how proud everyone was of him. "Hon, not a day went by after the accident where I didn't ask myself how a world could be so cruel as to take you from us. And now I see a world so miraculous and full of wonder that it could return you to us. I know it's not quite the same, but just seeing you and being with you means everything in the world to us. And when any normal kid would have bemoaned his fate and moped around the barn, you did what you always have—made the best of things and dedicated yourself to achieving everything you could."

Next it was Frank who stepped up and told his son much the same, adding that they would make every effort to see him as much as possible from now on. Frank had discussed with Melody the possibility of moving closer, and they both agreed to start looking for positions in the area. Petra would graduate in June, and although they would need to discuss it with Alison, they were pretty sure she'd be okay moving schools if it meant being closer to her brother.

Petra came over to give Hal a hug and kiss and simply said "Way to go bro'!" Alison was last and held onto Hal's head for a long time and told him that as soon as he was done racing he could have his old room back and they could play air hockey again. Hal himself was overcome with mixed emotions, so grateful to have his family back again but sad that he had no way to communicate his feelings to them without an intermediary.

As they were driving back to their hotel, Melody finally let everyone in on her little secret, at least in part. "Slight change of plans, guys. We are staying an extra day. We have another important event to attend!"

CHAPTER THIRTY-EIGHT

When they arrived back at the hotel, the first thing Frank Carmody did was to find ESPN on the TV so that they could watch endless replays of the race, along with all the accolades from the reporters. Normally Frank was the only one who watched the sports news channel, but on this night they were all happy to sit and watch replay after replay while dining on overpriced room service fare. While Frank and the girls were riveted to the set, Melody dug deep into her suitcase to find the formal outfits she had packed for them.

On the other side of town, Eleanor was doing pretty much the same thing. Of course she and Sid had won some money betting on Necromancer, and they celebrated at a local eatery, not fancy but good and plentiful food, ribs and chicken and corn on the cob and cherry cobbler for dessert. When she presented to Sid his best suit and a pair of freshly polished shoes, he asked her what this was for. She replied, "Well, you want to look good for your wedding, don't you?" Sid took a step back and said "Wait a minute, you told me the wedding was being postponed because we couldn't find anywhere in Lexington to have it!" "Slight change of plans, sweetie. A mutual friend managed to help out in that regard. And there is quite a story to go with it!"

Eleanor proceeded to tell Sid the story that Melody had told her the day they met at the supermarket. When she finished and looked up, she was shocked to see tears streaming from Sid's eyes. When she asked him what was wrong, he held a finger up and went to get some tissues to blow his nose and wipe his eyes. After composing himself, he said, "Nothing's wrong. I just can't believe it. Of all the bizarre things, the boy I helped kill comes back to save my life. When I was in my darkest days, I often thought about what a twisted sense of humor God possessed. But even I couldn't have imagined anything like this. Do you think he somehow knew that I owed him one and kept me around to save the girl?" Eleanor wasn't sure whether he meant the boy or the almighty, but she replied, "You best save that question for someone with a lot more wisdom than I possess. At this point, I'm pretty much in the 'anything's possible' camp. All I know is that a kind and loving man was saved and given to me, and that I couldn't be happier or prouder than I am to be marrying him tomorrow."

During one of the commercial breaks, Melody asked for everyone's attention and said "You will each find in the closet an outfit for tomorrow. We have a wedding to attend, and, yes, Petra, I actually mean it this time." She waved off questions about who and where and told them they would find out tomorrow.

The next day, the family was again met by a hired car and they piled in, with only Melody knowing their destination. Mr. Jenkins had been kind enough to also arrange a car for Sid and Eleanor. As they approached Holyrood, the Carmodys saw that decorations and tables had been laid out everywhere, and there was a stand set up with flowers adorning each side. A priest was milling about, chatting with guests, who had lemonade and tea and stronger drinks for those with the fortitude at ten in the morning. About fifty chairs had been set up in front of the stand for the wedding guests. They spotted Martha and Leroy Jenkins and Stevie, who looked adorable in a blue and white striped dress. Melody went over to those three and commented how gorgeous everything looked and how much she appreciated them doing this for Sid and Eleanor. Leroy said, "Well, I won't lie to you. Getting all this ready the day after the Derby was no small feat. And while I'm sure that Sid and Eleanor are fine people, this was done for you and your family, including your son." Stevie smiled shyly and exchanged quick hugs with everyone.

Per arrangements, the driver for Sid and Eleanor called Mr. Jenkins when they were about ten minutes from the farm. Mrs. Jenkins corralled everyone and got them to their seats, and had someone inside the house get the music ready so it could be piped outside. As the car pulled up and Sid and Eleanor got out, everyone stood up and gave them a rousing round of applause. Sid looked like a deer in the headlights, and Eleanor had a wide smile. As she crooked her arm into Sid's and they began walking towards the stand, Here Comes the Bride began playing on the loudspeaker. They reached the stand and Sid suddenly realized in a panic that they had no rings. As he began to motion to Eleanor she opened her other hand to reveal two wedding bands. For about the millionth time he thought to himself how unbelievably lucky he was to have found this woman.

After the ceremony, a small band came out and played standard wedding fare, while waiters came around with trays of fancy-looking nibbles. After some dancing and drinks and lots of introductions and congratulations, lunch was served. As Sid had no best man, Leroy Jenkins volunteered to do the toast. "Sid and Eleanor, although we've never met before today, I've heard an awful lot about you. And it's all been good. For a select few of you, there is a story that surrounds this wedding that defies belief, and yet we know it to be true. With everything that has happened to bring not only the two of you together, but all of us, I can't help but think that the two of you will have a long and blessed marriage." Shouts of "Cheers" followed the toast, and Sid got up and quieted everyone down. "Mr. and Mrs. Jenkins, words cannot begin to express my gratitude for what you have done for us today. I'll leave that for my much more eloquent wife. And Mrs. Carmody, you know I owe you more than I could ever begin to repay you. They say that everything happens for a reason, and I used to think that was just some sentimental nonsense, but let me tell you, I believe it now with everything in my heart. And if I could take it all back I would, you know that. But I'm glad that I can't. I know that may sound selfish, but I couldn't imagine living another day without this incredible woman by my side."

This evoked another round of "Cheers" along with several bouts of tears, not the least of which came from Eleanor. After the rest of the toasts and the serving of coffee and cake, Leroy Jenkins rose one more time and announced. "Now, I have one more surprise for everyone here. It's not often that you get a celebrity of this stature to come to a wedding on short notice, and I had to pull a lot of strings to get it done. But now, let me introduce to you..."

Hearing her cue, Stevie led Necromancer from the side of the house, wearing his Kentucky Derby blanket and groomed to the nth degree. Everyone rose and loudly applauded the heroic horse, and those that could made loud whistles. Stevie let go of the lead and Necromancer trotted over to where Sid and Eleanor stood and did as close to a bow as a horse could, and everyone laughed and cheered. As he went up tentatively to pat the horse's nose, this horse that had saved his life, he could have sworn he heard the horse thank him for saving his sister. So he whispered in the horse's ear "thank you for saving my life." And Necromancer simply nodded. He went back over to where Stevie was waiting, let her climb aboard, and they raced off to the trees and wind and freedom they both cherished.

THE END

ABOUT THE AUTHOR

Jay Tuckerman is the author of *Ruffian*. He lives in New York City with his wife Hilary. He is an author, lawyer, animal rights advocate and volunteer.